I0535153

IN LOVING MEMORY OF
ALLANTE' LAMONT LIGHTFOOT
AKA "ALLA"
JANUARY 3, 1989 – FEBRUARY 12, 2005

MYRON JAMES ARMSTRONG JR.
AKA "LUMP"
JANUARY 15, 1998 – FEBRUARY 21, 2014

MELVIN DAMACIO FOSTER
AKA "MELVO"
JUNE 21, 1995 – JUNE 28, 2015

WE'RE GOING TO ALWAYS HOLD YOUR MEMORY
DOWN

LOVE ALWAYS YOUR FATHERS

ANTONIO LIGHTFOOT
&
MYRON ARMSTRONG SR.

Acknowledgements

God the Father, and Christ my Savior, THANK YOU for allowing me to experience life. Deborah L. Huy-Green, THANK YOU for being the one God used to give me life. I love you Ma. Evon Williams, THANK YOU so much for your love and support. Arraja, Andre, Antonio Lightfoot Jr, Tracie Williams, Scarlett, and all of my nieces and nephews, Amy, and the rest of the family, there are too many names for me to get you all but there are more books to come. I LOVE YOU and THANK YOU all. I'll get you all next time. Forgive me.

Clifton J Washington-Deuce. Thank you for your hands and fingers. You typed your ass off. I appreciate you. Myron Armstrong-B.G., it all started with me messing around with you. Now look, I truly appreciate what you did for me. Thank you. I'm grateful.

Mrs. Norma Armstrong. I love you spirit. Thank you for your optimism. Heather Brown aka Beautiful. This book started with a picture of you…You see what impact you had. I'm eternally grateful that God allowed me to meet you. All the props you get, you deserve. I told you in the email, I run the Heather Brown Fan Club. LOL! Team 13 Publications. Let's go! Street Consequences Magazine, let's go!

"Yeah, you niggas think this shit is a game a game that is until you get caught and then it's serious ain't it... Guess what nigga it was serious all the time."

****

A mallet slams and the judge begins…

"You may be seated, Mr. Roi, is the defendant ready?"
"Yes, you Honor."
"Will the defendant stand." Once the defendant stands the judge continues. "Mr. Light, I'm perplexed because while I have had plenty of people in this very courtroom who have done greater harm to society, yet have received far less than the mandatory sentence that I'm about to impose on you, nevertheless, you are a danger. I truly believe that you could have been anything that you chose and I have no doubt that you chose this life. While I acknowledge the overwhelming amount of support that I see represented for you in this room you will never see society again.

I hereby sentence you to a period of LIFE imprisonment without the possibility of parole. Bailiff, take him away…."

SCENE 1:
CUBS ON THE PROWL

"Allante', get in here!" yelled his mother. "Aiight Slim, I got to go. I'll holler at y'all tomorrow. I got something I need to talk with him about too." Said Allante' to his best friend Lump. "Aiight Alla, we'll see you tomorrow fool." responded Lump. Allante' disappeared into his mother's house.

"Look boy, I need you to help me out around here." Said his mother "Aiight Ma."
"I work hard Alla, and when I come home I'm tired and I expect you to watch your brothers."
"I got you Ma."
"I know you don't have the life of other kids and I'm sorry for that, but I'm doing this by myself."
"I got'em Ma. I love you!"

Turning back to his friends Allante' continues, "I said that would never happen again, and Mo, I ain't gonna ever let these weak azz niggas purp on us talking bout they put us on. We gon get our own shit and we gon get rich, are y'all wit me?" Lump and Melvo nodded, "Plus we equal y'all know me, I don't let people get close to me, but if I fuck wit you then you my family…"

Looking with excitement, both brothers said, "Yeah Mo, we wit you, fuck these niggas out here let's go."

"I know y'all be seeing shit out here and be looking like that nigga ain't supposed to have this and that… well I see this nigga every day, driving his Benz riding through here and I'm tired of seeing it… I got a plan."

****

1 WEEK LATER

"Melvo, when I get this nigga in the house I want you got to go upstairs and check all the rooms, closets and under the beds to make sure ain't nobody else in there."

"Lump you come in and check the entire lower level… the kitchen, family room and basement and don't take them gloves off or your mask off and don't say our names." Allante' onced them over to make sure they understood his instructions. "My word to y'all we coming out of this. I know his schedule so we got to get this nigga Thursday night…" said Allante'.

1:30 a.m.
THURSDAYMORNING

"What the FUCK!"

"The first bullet gon go through the back of yo head, and open yo face up now shut the fuck up and open the door and be quiet nigga!" growled Allante'. "Let's go y'all… sit on the floor nigga and don't talk unless I tell you too and I'm only gon tell you that one time. Fuck around with me and play games if you want and I'mma kill yo azz. Look at me, I don't do no faking!" Allante' grips on his prey.

"Aye slim, she was upstairs sleep, she the only one!" "Alright." responds Allante'. "Everything else clear." said Lump walking from the basement back into the living room while Melvo brings the girls down the steps.

"What's your name Shorty?"
"Carla…" she replied shaking.
"Take her over there." Allante' looks at their victim whose sitting on the floor petrified. "Nigga you got one time to tell me where money and drugs at and just know that if you lie I'mma hurt both of y'all, so where is it at?" Sitting on the floor looking up at the masked robbers the victim begins to talk. "You too young for this lil nigga… you don't--- SMACK! Allante' slaps him across the head with the barrel of his .9 millimeter.
"I ain't average!" said Allante.
Turning the woman… "You said your name Carla, right?" asked Allante, "I'm gon ask you one time Carla, where is the money and the drugs?"

"If you lie to me and we find anything you didn't tell us about I'mma hurt you for lying, plus he already said that he don't give a fuck about you... so one time, where is it?"

She nodded frantically and stuttered. "Heeee he guhh got money in the pillows of the couch, it's some stashed under the washing machine and under the bottom drawer in the Chest of drawer set.". He nodded. "Where the drugs at?" "They in the closet in the room with the PlayStation." Turning to his partners, Allante' asked, "Y'all got that?" He turns to Carla, "Aye yo why is you wit this bitch azz nigga... he said fuck you!"

5 MINUTES LATER

"A Mo, we got that!" yelled Lump. "Aiight! Y'all go ahead I'm right behind y'all!" Still sitting on the floor with a look of disgust on his face the victim stares up at the masked men. He begins speaking. "Look man, you got what you came for."

"Yeah nigga, but it didn't come from you like it was supposed to it came from her... see a real nigga, if he got it once... he can get it again. Family is most important and you know what you are... a ghost... you just the last one to know you dead."

"If you shoot that gun you gon wake up my neighbors…."
"Yeah you smart and that's why I got this knife cause you don't deserve a bullet! I want you to see what death look like." Allante' pauses from speaking to lift his mask from over his face. "You ride through here like you the shit nigga and you right… you are shit but you know what shit is?", he and Allante' were almost nose to nose. "It's what the body gets' rid of when it don't have no use for it anymore!"

Allante' has his gun pointed at the victim in one hand and with the other he quickly thrust the knife repeatedly into the victim's neck, head, and face causing him to scream out in agony while blood spurts everywhere covering the walls and floor. Placing the mask back down over his face Allante' walks into the other room where the woman Carla is sitting crying uncontrollably. Using the bloody knife Allante' begins to cut the extension cord from her ankles and wrists.

"Your boy is dead! Don't end up like him, choose your boyfriends more wisely from now on cause you got a future but he doesn't. You didn't see our faces, so when the police come just tell the truth." They left Carla there in the home unharmed closing the door behind them.

THE NEXT DAY
10:30 a.m.

"Slim, we got $137,000.00 plus we got thirty pounds of loud and a brick of coke." beamed Allante'. "How you do that Alla, how you know?" asked Melvo. "Look at him Mo… cause he wanted everybody to know he got it. Some shit is cool to get you know clothes and some jewelry, but you can't go crazy. We got to help others get up too; we can't become the same thing we hate."

****

"This morning on the 11 o'clock news, one-man is killed in a suspected drug robbery. While all the details are not yet in the victim was viscously stabbed to death but there was another person present who was unharmed; we will follow up later with more details today…", announced the female news reporter form the Detroit news station.

Looking at the television inside of Lump and Melvo's house, Lump begins, "Damn Mo, you wet him up…"
"Mo, I told y'all I ain't like that nigga. I ain't let that broad see me cook him plus he ain't have no respect for what we was doing. He played with his life but this shit is real life… just always remember that the same shit we do to these niggas they can do to us if we out here slipping." Allante' continues, "We got to have a plan y'all…"

Melvo turned the T.V. off with his remote control. They are all sitting inside of him and Lump's bedroom.
"Alla we only sixteen years old man… we ain't got no plan."
"Then we gon start making one for instance I gotta figure out a way to help my mother cause I can't just give her no money she ain't gon take it."

Allante' looked around the room at their caper, "This shit don't mean nothing if we can't lift our family up with it… we gon split this money thirty thousand apiece, and we gon put $47,000.00 in the pot… now with the loud we going to help our boys in the neighborhood with, and that brick we need to make every dollar out of it." Allante smiled," We gon put our hood on the map Mo, we more than friends…we family and we gon come up together, we gon take care of our mothers and we gon own some shit!"

Lump cuts in, "What we gon own, we too young? "Allante' looks at his friend confidently.
"But we ain't gon be young forever." said Allante', Lump smiling adds, "I want a clothing store."
"How about you own clothes, make niggas wear shit with your name on it now that's some real shit." Allante' spoke matter-of-factly.

Melvo said, "I want a Car Lot so we can start selling used cars from the repo auctions all we need is somebody to buy them for us."

"I want to get some houses and own some of that shit downtown all that abandoned shit on the riverfront down there could be turned into a goldmine!"

Looking at the ceiling in deep thought he turned to his friends "I'mma buy something… I ain't gon ever go broke again without a doubt." finished Allante'. "Yeah man bet!" Allante' rubbed his hands together, and said, "Look Mo, I love y'all and I want for y'all what I want for myself so I'mma let y'all know though, this shit right here ain't enough, we just getting started."

****

Detective Bernice Campbell is a caramel brown woman, 5'6 feet tall and weighs about 140 pounds, she has sandy brown hair that hangs down just past her shoulders. At the age of twenty-seven she has been working on the Detroit homicide squad for two years. She's sitting inside of her work office listening to her co-worker.

"Campbell, we don't have any leads on the descriptions of the suspects, we just know that it was three black males. We don't have any complexions, their heights were between 5'5 and 5'8 and the surviving victim said she believed the suspects were young, like between eighteen and nineteen years old. She said they seemed like they knew what they were doing and none of them touched her in any sexual way…"

"That's rare, all of these weak perverts out here. But they really did a number on this guy like killing him was personal." answered Campbell.
Her partner Brooks is a 5'9, twenty-seven-year-old black male with a stocky build.

"Campbell the girl said that the shortest one took control. She said he told the other two to go ahead and leave like he as making sure they got away first and he is the one who killed her boyfriend after the other two had left."

"Sounds like we have a protector in the crew and he might also be the most dangerous… did we get any finger-prints?"
"None. The girl said that they all had on black leather gloves." Campbell smiles at him. "They ain't stupid this one might take a while Brooks."

****
LATER THAT NIGHT

"Ma!"
"What?"
"I'm trying to buy the Cutlass from you."

"How are you gon pay for it Allante'?"
"I'll get a job; plus, you know I'm about to graduate." Allante' smiled from ear to ear.
"Yeah, but you have to also have car insurance."
"You already took me to get my license and that's the car I want."
"We'll see."
"I love you Ma!"
"I love you too, I had you when I was sixteen years old Allante'." she smiled.
"And you are the love of my life Ma.

I'm going to bed now cause I got to go train tomorrow then I got a fight on Saturday…. oh yeah here go some money Ma."
"Allante', this is $500.00, where you get this?"
"Me, Lump, and Melvo helped this man work on this house and he paid us."
"Thank you."
"We suppose to help him on some other stuff, so I'mma take Arraja and Andre shopping; I got you Ma!"
"You know you graduating!"
"I know Ma, I just want to take care of you."

"Allante', I've worked since I was thirteen years old. When I retire, I will have over ninety-percent of my pay-check. I'll be okay son. You take care of yourself."
"I want to buy you a bigger house and whatever kind of car you want. You are my mother and my

father and it ain't supposed to be like that. You take care of me, Arraja, and Andre and ain't nobody taking care of you."

"Allante', God has never not given me what I wanted, I'm fine."

"I really look up to you Ma."

****

Allante' is upstairs at his little brothers' bedroom door standing in the doorway. "What's up y'all?" "Allante' can you please tell Arraja to give me my stuff back." said Andre from where he sits across from Arraja on the bedroom floor. "Take your stuff back." said Allante' "It's not his its mines." Arraja said with attitude.

"Hold up, first of all y'all ain't supposed to be fighting over nothing, you suppose to help him and both of y'all supposed to help Mama y'all don't ever supposed to fight over things do you hear me?". "Yeah.". They respond in unison looking up at their big brother.

"Arraja, that's you lil brother don't ever let me find out you ain't looking out for him and Andre the same thing for you." nodding they agreed with Allante', "Okay.". "Good,
I'mma take y'all shopping tomorrow."
"Yeahhhh!" both boys responded in excitement. "I got y'all!"

SATURDAY 1:30 P.M

"Look Allante' work his body, then his head, get off first!" Yelling through his face mask, "I got him coach... I'mma crush him! The bell rings! The commentator announces with excitement, "Allante' Light is a very promising prospect coming out of Kronks Boxing Gym and he really is the whole package!"

"He moves good and has such vision just look at him... perfect jab to the body, left upper cut, left hook, ohh! He has Johnson dazed! Eww... Light hits him wit a straight right to the jaw, oh my GOODNESS LIGHT SQUATTED DOWN, and hit Johnson with a right-hand body shot and it folded Johnson, he's on his knees!"

Commentator two joins in, "I don't think he's getting back up! He just stopped the fight with a body shot in the first round."
"I'm telling you this kid could go pro right now! I don't see anybody stopping him!" said commentator one.

****

"Son, you're good!" said the coach. "Aye Coach I'm ready! I want to turn pro!"
"Give me a couple more of fights, we'll see when you turn seventeen."

"Anything could happen between then and now... Allante' you have your whole life ahead of you! Just be patient."

****

NORTHLAND MALL
6 p.m.

"Alla you beat the fuck out of that nigga! He couldn't fuck with you at all Mo! Shit, I need to be in the gym with you... you think I could do it?" Melvo added, "Dawg you a beast! You made that nigga quit! I can tell you gon make it! I can see it in your eyes Alla, you love that shit and you a natural!"

"Did y'all see all those bitches there?" asked Lump. "Damn, Alla they was talking bout you too straight dick ridin when you went in the ring and how you folded that nigga up!" Lump was acting animated azz fuck hoping all around Allante' he put his hands on his shoulders, "Man I heard one of the broads say she wanted to suck yo dick!" he laughed.

Melvo then said, "Get the fuck out of here." Lump smiled, "No bullshit, one girl said you could fuck her in her ass, if you fuck as good as you can fight."

"It's always broads at the fights and at the gym I ain't found that one yet." Allante' said shaking his head. "Shit, they all that one, Alla." said

Melvo. "They the one, two, three, and four fa sho."
Lump laughed. Melvo continues, "I'll fuck all them
bitches."

"Nigga, you ain't even fucking yet so you
don't even know what to do with no pussy." said
Lump. "I caught this nigga jacking off last week,"
Lump continued, I scared him and shit was flying
everywhere you be sure you make that nigga wash
his hands before he give you a dap."

The mall is crowded as they walk side by side
to the Lord & Taylor store and Allante' spoke,
"Let's go in Lord & Taylors, you know I need that
fly shit..." "Y'all be spending a lot of money on
this shit." said Lump. Melvo said, "Nigga we love
to put them pieces on, right Alla?"

Allante' nodded and rubbed his hands
together "My mother kept me in that fly shit, I'm
just following tradition." Unfazed Lump went on
with his commentary trying to prove his point.
"I mean, that shit is cool but y'all be putting too
much thought into that shit." said Lump. "First
impression Mo, I'm always ready to make that first
impression the best impression." said Allante'.

Melvo looks at Allante', "He don't know
about that shit, look at him Alla, Bama azz nigga."
They all laugh walking to the clothes racks. "Man,

fuck y'all…I know how to dress." Lump looks down unsure of his outfit.

"Aye Mo, y'all see them broads over there?" asked Allante'.
"Where?"
"Over there at the counter."
"Mannn them dusty azz skinny bitches. Them bitches look hungry like they want to eat a muthafucka." They all laughed. Lump continued, "They look thirsty and they window shopping."
"Slim, we use to be window shoppers." said Allante'. "Man, I ain't buying no bitches nothing and I ain't saving no hoes.' said Lump.
"Where that come from?"

"I'm talking bout potential pussy, y'all talking about tricking, you see the one in the middle, Shorty laying like that, I'm trying to get that." said Allante'. Two of the females they're speaking about who are browsing through some clothes look back to see Lump, Allante' and Melvo approaching them.

"Hello there beautiful," began Allante' with a smile. The girls all began giggling shyly. "Excuse me but can I talk to you for a minute? I know you with your friends and all but I need to holler at you." said Allante'. "Shit you can holler at me." answered one of the girls out of the three. "Nawl sweetheart, I'm trying to talk to beautiful, you know who you are, in the middle, BROWN SUGAR."

"Hmph!" The girls wave their friend in the middle off both smirking. "Girl go ahead… we right here."

"What's your name love?" asked Allante' Walking off with the girl to the side. "Love?" "Don't worry it's just an expression and a good one but if you tell me your name I won't have to call you Love or Beautiful even though it fits you well" said Allante' causing her to smile from ear to ear.

"My name is Heather." Rubbing his hands together. "Heather?" a beautiful name for a beautiful girl." Allante' continues to admire her. "Why you keep calling me beautiful?" "If you could see what I see you'd call yourself beautiful too…" "My name is Allante', and I need you to be mines." "Boy, you don't even know me." "I know me and I wouldn't have pulled up on you if I was willing to let you get away." "So what that mean?" "I'm used to getting what I want." "It ain't that easy." "It ain't supposed to be, but I like what I see." "And?" "I'm trying to see more… look, I know you with your girls so can I call you?" "I don't play games." "Beautiful, you already mines." "You think you the shit."

Allante' laughs. "Nawl, I think you're the shit." Suddenly a stranger walks up with a look of excitement and says, "Excuse me ain't you Allante' Light? I saw your fight earlier today, you looked really good in the ring today son, stick with it and you're going to go far!"

"Thank you." answered Allante' and the man walked off.

"You be boxing?"

"Yeah."

"I like that."

"Well give me your number, and I can teach you how to fuck."

"Did you just say-

"I mean fight." laughed Allante'.

Heather smirks at him, before reaching in her hobo sack for her phone to exchange numbers. "I just wanted to see you smile that's why I said that." Meanwhile, Allante's two little brothers who were running around in the toy store found their way into the Lord & Taylors. "Allante' we hungry." said his little brothers in unison. "Aiight, we'll go to Coney Island."

"Who is this?" asked Heather.

"These are my little brothers, say hey to beautiful."

"Hey Beautiful." the brothers say in unison.

"That's not my name."

"That's my name for you, I'll call you later…Thank you." said Allante' to Heather.

"For What?"

"Making my day."

Heather smiles brightly, and Allante' said, "There you go with that pretty azz smile again. You wear it well."

Melvo and Lump walk up when Heather and her girls are walking out of the store. "Dawg you got her, she looking back at you and all them bitches giggling." said Lump. "Yeah but Shorty ain't no bitch though I like her...I can just tell it's something about her."

"She fine Alla, I ain't gone front." said Melvo. "What's up with her friends?" asked Lump "Nigga, you ain't holla at none?" asked Allante'.

"I thought you was setting it up."

"Picture that, you on your own nigga, now let's shop so I can get my little brothers something to eat."

SATURDAY NIGHT
10 p.m.

Laying on her bed watching T.V., Heather's phone begins to ring.

She reaches over to the dresser picking up her cell phone.

"Hello?"

"Can I speak to Heather?"

"This me."

"Hey Beautiful."

"Hey."

"I been thinking about you all day."

21

"Why me?"

"Why not you?" He then began to add; "That pretty brown skin and you got that perfect face to wear that short hair-cut, you know you got that body...you sexy azz hell. When I saw you, I don't know... I couldn't take my eyes off you. I want you..."

"You don't even know me."

"Heather, nobody knows anybody until they give them a chance."

"True."

"Let me know you, tell me something about yourself."

"I like to do hair."

"Can you do mines?"

"I could hook you up, I can do any kind of hair."

"My barber gone be mad when I cut him off."

"But I'mma hook you up doe!"

"You saying my shit ain't right?"

"I'm saying I got that touch."

"I bet you do."

"You silly."

"You fine!" He then continues, "So tell me something else."

"I don't have time for games, niggas be on some dumb shit all immature and lying and shit. Just say what you mean and keep shit real."

"Look, you stood out from your girls. I got a beautiful mother and she raised me and my brothers all by herself. I respect all black women including you so if you let me I'm taking you all the way."

22

"What that mean?"

"We gon grow old together."

"You just want some pussy."

"Shorty believe me, I don't have to try hard to get that, I been getting that for a long time and I just understand better now."

"What you mean by that?"

"We'll talk about it face to face."

"Alright."

"I'm gon get off this phone now, I called you, now my number in your phone, call me."

"What you laying down play?"

"Nawl, I'm just telling you what I expect."

"Where you from? You different."

"I ain't trying to be the same."

****

3 DAYS LATER
LUMP AND MELVO'S HOUSE

"Mo, I think I got another lick." said Allante'

"What up doe?" asked Melvo.

"Over on Lilac, I keep seeing these Mexicans go in and out of this house."

"Mexicans?"

"Yeah… and they ain't supposed to be over here it's only dudes and they be gone for days at a time." Lump cuts in, "How you know?"

"Cause I be watching shit, you know I get up and go running at 4:30 in the morning so I see shit moving around when everybody else be sleep and they got shit in there guaranteed… I just don't know what it is."

"So, what we gon do?"

"I'm going up in there tonight." said Allante' matter-of-factly. Lump then asked, "and what we gon do?"

"Be ready."

"I'm going with you."

"Nawl, let me go, and when I get in if its good then I'll call y'all in… one person is less movement if ain't nothing in there I can get out faster but if something's there then I'll get y'all in quicker."

"Bet." said Melvo.

Lump then added, "Alla, I love you Slim."

"We family, I told y'all we gon get rich."

****

4:30 a.m.
WEDNESDAY

Allante' walks in the dark around the back of the house on Lilac dressed in all black with a hoodie over his head. Stopping at the basement window he places his hands to lift it up, finding that it isn't locked it comes right up and he climbs right inside easily.

Inside its quiet, he creeps up the basement stairs reaching the top he opens the door, and is met by the growl of a dog. Instantly he reacts retrieving his knife thrusting it into the dog's neck making the dog whimper collapsing as it tries to back away. Making his way through the house, he notices a Mexican man sleeping on the living room couch with the T.V. loud.

Making his way up the steps he begins to check every room one by one breathing a sigh of relief as he realizes that there is no one else inside of the home. In the master bedroom, his eyes grew wide… JACKPOT!

Allante' walks slowly back down the steps, with his knife in his hand that has blood of the dog he killed still on it. He walks around to the sleeping man on the couch and thrusts the knife into his neck forcefully over and over with blood spurting everywhere, the man shakes before taking his last breath when the knife is planted in his jugular vein.

Allante' pulls his cell phone from his pocket calling Lump and Melvo. "Come to the back of the house I'll be at the back door."
"Got you!" Moments later, both Lump and Melvo dressed in black with their hoodies over their heads circle the back of the house once inside they enter the living room seeing the dead Mexican dead on the couch his body hanging halfway to the floor.

"Ayeeeee yo Slim, you ain't bullshitting!" said Melvo. "Hell nawl and from now on ain't nobody gon be able to live to talk about nothing!"

Allante' spoke with caution, "I ain't killing no black women and I ain't killing no kids, but we crushing dogs, cats, parrots, rabbits, and niggas.

C'mon, look at this shit!" They walked up the stairs to the master bedroom with Allante' in the lead. Melvo and Lumps eyes become wide as a deer being caught in headlights. "Damn! Look at all this shit!" The brothers couldn't believe their eyes.

"What the fuck, Dawg, look at all this shit!" said Melvo. "We rich!" added Lump, "How we gon get all this shit… we can't carry it?"
"We gon take what we can, that's all we can do, I told y'all they had some shit up in here so let's get this shit!"

Inside of the room is stacks upon stacks of kilograms of cocaine along wit stacks of money… it's actually a Mexican main stash house! "Get them bags over there and put as much money in them as you can Lump and Melvo I want some of them Ki's as well." instructed Allante'.
"We don't need the coke Alla."
"We taking some of all this shit just don't take them gloves off!" Melvo and Lump proceeded to pack two big gym bags with money and Allante' had two gym bags he filled to the top wit kilos.

Twenty minutes later, the three of them are heading out of the door. On their way out a car pulled up into the driveway with two Mexicans inside. "Dammit!" huffed Allante, "Aye y'all put the gym bags down, and stay on the steps." Allante' took up his post behind the front door and the moment that the Mexicans walked in he placed his .9mm to their heads; the black Glock looked very pretty in his hand aimed at them. "Don't say shit or I'mma blow your brains out! Sit the fuck down right here... Aye y'all, come'ere hurry up."

Melvo and Lump made their way to Allante'. "Go snatch that cord off that lamp and off that music system. Hurry up... tie these niggas up...." One of the Mexican began, "Yo homez who the fuck-Smack! Allante' hit him wit the barrel of his gun. "Shut the fuck up! Slim get those keys." "What we gon to do now?" asked Melvo. "We gon to get more of that shit upstairs now that we have a car."

"Fool you layin' like that!" said Lump. "Y'all take care of that and I'mma take care of them. Don't make a lot of noise when y'all go out to the car cause I don't want to wake up the neighbors around here and I don't want people seeing us leaving." "Got you." responded Melvo.

Allante' pulls out his knife and with his gun in his other hand and he manages to begin stabbing one of the Mexicans ruthlessly. The other Mexican knew that he or his friend didn't stand a chance.

Melvo and Lump make their last trip outside after looking at the bloody Mexicans who are both soon to be dead now that Allante' has begun knifing the other Mexican down to the floor; blood spurting everywhere. Soon they are driving away from the scene.

"Why you kill em?" asked Melvo from the backseat. "Cause now they can't tell they partners what we look like." answered Allante' looking back at Melvo. "Man fuck them, they ain't supposed to be in our neighborhood anyways.' said Allante'.

"Why you always putting in the work?" asked a curious faced Lump from the passenger seat. "Cause I don't want y'all to go through what I go through in my head if y'all don't have to I don't want y'all to do it... I got it."

****

BACK AT LUMP AND MELVO'S HOUSE

"Fool, we got not one... not two... but three nigga three fucking million two-hundred and sixty-five thousand dollars and eighty goddamn bricks; we fuckin rick!" said Lump. They all burst out into laughter sitting in Melvo and Lumps room. "We got that real lick." said Allante'. "Alla, look at this shit we some young niggas paid!!!" yelled Melvo.

"Yeah, now we can take our time." said Allante' "What you mean?" asked Lump. "I mean we got money now but that's three bodies for the police and three missing from a crew for the Mexicans. We got to be cool." said Allante'. He continued, "We gon sit back, go to school and plan what we gone do and how we gon do it just like you said Lump... we rich Dawg and if we do it right Mo...we gone get richer!"

"We ain't struggling no more but we can't be what we hate. Niggas who only look out for themselves and in time we gon look out for all our boys. We not gon be the same as those other lame azz niggas Mo, we gon be different. I love y'all. I'm going home...I'll see y'all tomorrow, we gon leave this shit here wit y'all till tomorrow. I left the car on Woodward and 7 Mile so we good."
"Alla we love the fuck out you."
"We family... I'll kill the world for y'all."

****

A FEW DAYS LATER
HEATHER'S HOUSE

A woman makes her way to the door, as someone is ringing the bell. She opens the door. "Hello Mrs. Brown, how are you doing... is Heather here?" asked Allante'. Turning her head Mrs. Brown calls out, "Heather, you have company... come on in baby."

"Thank you", responded Allante' stepping inside. "Have a seat in the living room, she'll be down in a minute." A little one-year old boy who's barely walking comes into the living room. "Hey… whussup lil man, come'ere…what's up with you." greeted Allante'.

He picked the little boy up and the little boy smiles at him. As Heather walks down into the room, seeing her Allante' stands up. He's holding the little boy. "Hey beautiful."
"Hey." answered Heather. "I was just playing with lil man, what's your name lil man?"
"His name is Josh." said Heather.
"Josh, you my friend."

The little boy smiles, Heather reaches out to grab him. "Come'ere boy." said Heather. "I got'em, right man." said Allante' he continued, "This your little brother?" asked Allante'. Heather answered "No, he's my son." Heather's news didn't faze Allante', she looks for a response. "That ain't surprise you?" asked Heather. "It don't change nothing, if that's what you mean."
"Me having a baby don't make you look at me different?"

"I mean, you still fine…your eyes and lips…they drive me crazy when I look at you."
"Boy, I mean, you still want me now?"

30

She then added. "I come with a package."
"Heather, my mother had me at sixteen years old and she is my biggest idol in this world and all that she achieved in this world she did it carrying me on her hip.

Allante' smiled at Josh as he spoke to Heather. "He makes me respect you more, not less." Turning to face her with a look of sincerity Allante continued," He ain't gon stop you from going anywhere if anything he's going to motivate you that much more to get there. Let me help you, ain't no strings attached to that."

"Why Allante? You could have any girl."
"Heather, I want you, I see you."
Heather stares deeply into his eyes, a tear rolls down her face. "It ain't easy raising him."
"I can help you make it easier."
"But he ain't yours." Allante' nods his head, "But he's apart of you, and I'm trying to make you mines.

He ain't done nothing wrong… he was born. Shorty, I really really like you." Allante' places his free arm around her shoulder.
"I got him and you."

****

**LATER THAT NIGHT
ALLANTE'S BEDROOM**

"I'm nervous." whispered Heather. "Nawl, you scared." Heather playfully punches him in his shoulder. "I'mma do it right beautiful; don't worry." Allante' begins by kissing her lips. Next, he kisses under her chin, then under her neck. Heather begins to relax, Allante' then opens her blouse and her bra is exposed.

Unbuttoning her jeans Allante' soon has her down to her black lace panties. Running his hands up and down her pretty brown thighs, he takes her shirt off. Kissing her shoulders and stomach while unsnapping her bra, her young pretty perky titties become exposed.

Heather's huge nipples are hard as shit. Allante' places his hand inside of her panties. Heather raises her butt up so that he can pull them down. She is now naked on his bed. On the CD player the song 'I Just want To Be your Girl' by Chapter 8 is playing. Allante' takes his shirt off, and his muscles protrude his body. She rubs her hands all over his chest then he continues to undress by taking off his pants and boxers, his dick is rock hard. Heather looks down at him, saying to herself in her head "Damn." He laid his body down between her legs able to feel her young heat.

Kissing her young lips again then their eyes lock and his mind is made up, this is going to be the best she ever had. He places her left nipple into his mouth, playing with it using his tongue knowing that she has never had it like he's about to give it to her. After sucking on her titties and nipples he trails kisses down to her stomach, then to her pubic hairs and she stops him.

"What are you doing?" asked Heather. Allante' realizes that no one has ever ate her box, so he said, "I'mma take you there." Feeling vulnerable, Heather laid back closing her eyes, allowing herself to get lost. Allante' slides down pushing her thighs apart blowing on her pretty brown pussy lips. Heather begins gasping, "Damn, he hasn't even started yet."

Allante' softly places his lips against her pussy lips, kissing them, licking out his tongue he softly French kisses her pussy, he gently pushes back her pussy lips and her young clit is exposed. Taking the tip of his wet tongue, he makes circles using his tongue on her clit, she unconsciously places both of her hands on his head.

Allante' smiles circling her clit with his tongue…first to the right, then to the left, next up and down, she starts getting wetter grinding her hips up into his face. The more he licks the wetter she becomes moaning throwing her hips up into his face. He sticks his finger into her ass while softly blowing in her pussy, her body begins to jerk. She feels strange and moaned out, "Eww shit!" She began cumming, her first ever orgasm in her sixteen years of life.

Sliding his body up between her legs, he places the head of his dick into her pussy slowly pushing up inside of her. She gasps the further he slides inside of her. Opening her legs wider to take more of him in, she now knows what real love feels like. She understands now that she has more to give and she wants to give it all to him.

Heather plants her feet firmly on the bed throwing her hips up, down and around matching every stroke that Allante' throws. She whispers in his ear, "Fuck me, I belong to you." He takes his time with her, and this drives her crazy, she orgasmed for the second time, and didn't know that sex could be so good. After awhile his strokes became faster and harder she could feel his dick pulsating like it was going to explode and just like that she could feel him cumming inside of her. She wrapped her legs and arms around him even tighter and didn't let go.

THE NEXT DAY
HEATHER AND HER GIRLFRIENDS AT SCHOOL

"I don't know what the hell he did to my body it felt so damn good my body was shaking and shit.

He licked my pussy and made me cum and then he fucked me and made me cum."

"Damn, I'm jealous…bitch these niggas don't know how to fuck all they want to do is bust a nut but it sounds like Alla the truth; I wonder if that nigga Lump know what he doing." said Keisha. "Shit and his brother Melvo too…the friends gave each other a high-five "ALRIGHT", all of them be fresh and I like that they stick together." I like that too…but I thought they was all related?" ended Bree. Heather cuts in, "Allante' from D.C., his mother moved up here when he was nine years old."

"I knew he was different, shit I'm going down there." said Keisha. "Right bitch. Maybe they all like that." added Bree. She then rolled her neck asking them, "You think…. Hell nawl."
"Lump and Melvo from Memphis, they came up here with they mother just like Alla but he three of them like brothers forreal." said Heather. "Shit, we need to hook up with the other two so say something to Alla and see what's up." said Keisha. "
Bitch if it don't work I don't want to hear no shit from y'all." said Heather. "I need some good dick.

If it's half as good as what you got I'm good." laughed Bree. "Yeah bitch, these niggas out here ain't no damn good ole…K2 smoking azz motherfuckers, I'll let the pussy dry up before I give it to any of them." ended Keisha.

****

ALLANTE' HOUSE, 1 WEEK AFTER THE ROBBERY

"Fool, we got so much money and way too much coke, what we are going to do?" asked Melvo. Allante' gave him an intense glare and replied, "Melvo, we ain't got to do shit bro …we paid! We ain't spend all of the first money we got.

Look, I know it's hard but we can't change the police all around the hood. We ain't getting no cars or none of that yet, plus we gotta keep our ear to the ground and we gotta just listen to what niggas is talking about.

Pounding his fist into his hand to emphasize his point, "Real talk bro, the hardest thing is not getting the money it's keeping it!" "Don't nobody know what we know or do …check it we dress fly azz shit and we always got money in our pockets." Lump and Melvo nodded as he spoke. "Right now, all they know is sometimes we got that loud and we can sit on this shit forever we gone work out our plans together, aiight?" said Allante'. In agreement both brothers said "Alright."

"Mo, remember, we only sixteen and my mother sold me the cutlass for $500 so we got transportation, well figure the rest out. Let's go to Cedar Point next week, they'll opening for the summer." said Allante'. "Bet" answered the brothers in unison… "I'mma holler at Heather to get her girls to go with us."

"I'mma trying to fuck Keisha. She got a fat azz!" said Lump. "And Bree good to go too." said Melvo. "She might be too much for you." said Allante'. "Yeah, scared azz nigga. You know you ain't never had no pussy." said Lump laughing at Melvo. Fuck you nigga. It's a first time for everything." said Melvo.

****

DETROIT/ROBBERY/HOMOCIDE

"The Lilac Triple Homicide has the same method of murder as the one over by the University of Detroit. I think it's the same person or people; it seems to be one blade used on all of the victims and a witness saw three men leave the house around 5:30 a.m. in a gray Subaru Outback. We found one abandoned on Woodward and 7 Mile with no prints. Brooks, keep checking the neighborhood, somebody is going to slip up." said Detective Campbell. "Okay, but they left over two-hundred thousand dollars and twenty kilos… what were they thinking?" responded Brooks. "Not to get greedy, they're not stupid.

I'm surprised those Mexican lasted over there that long. According to the old lady next door they were in that house for months. They stuck out like gazelle hanging out in a Lion's pride but unfortunately for them somebody is a real killer and the witnesses in both incidents say they look young but the experience that it takes to pull these off without any mistakes makes me question if these guys aren't in their thirty's, I'm convinced they're pros. Something will come up. We just have to be patient after all… they are targeting drug dealers and I ain't mad at them.

CEDAR POINT; SANDUSKY, OHIO

"You scared of rollercoasters?" Allante' asked Heather. Heather laughs, "Not as long as you're beside me."
" I got your left side, right side, front and back." said Allante'. "Well as long as I got you I ain't scared of nothing… I'm falling for you Allante'."

"I'm falling for you more, Heather. You gone be my wife." Heather looked into his eyes. "Why you be looking at me like that?" asked Allante'.
"Like what?" she smiled. "Look girl, your eyes… man I swear I ain't never seen none like yours before ever in my life they are the most beautiful cause you are the most beautiful."
"Why you be saying that?"

"Heather, I wish you could see yourself from my eyes, you skin, your lips, your nose, your eyes, the way you wear your hair, your hips, ass, legs, breast, and the way you walk. You're a star Heather and you shine. I'm proud of you."

"For what?"

"Shorty, you're a good mother, you do your hair and keep yourself up and you pour all that you have into him."

"I need to get my cosmetology license, so I can open up my own shop someday." She said optimistically "I'll pay for the school, whenever you want to go.", said Allante'. "For real?" Heather squinted. "Heather, you are me so when I do for you and Josh, I'm doing for myself."

A tear is inside of Heather's eye. "Hey don't start that." Heather laughs at his comment. "I'm sorry. I don't know what I did to get you."

"As soon as we get old enough, I'm trying to marry you, and put a baby in you."

"You that dude."

"You make me feel like that dude when niggas see me holding your hand."

Heather laughs again.

"Alla, how did you pay for the bus to bring us all down here and pay for the hotel room?" She continued, "You brought the whole neighborhood down here."

"Me, Lump, and Melvo put our money together, it ain't never all me. They got they own money."

"But where you get the money from?" Heather continued, "Look, I don't care, I think you be hustling, but it ain't gon stop me from loving you, I'm your down azz bitch. You love my son like he's yours, you take care of us, and you give me money to help my mother out. But let's be clear it ain't about the money, I know you love me, and you always lift me up, I need you to do one thing for me."

"What's that baby?"

"Please be careful, my heart couldn't take losing you."

"I mean that much to you?"

"Boy don't play with me, and I need you to do what you did with your tongue tonight."

"What I do?"

"Licky licky."

"I don't know what you talking about."

She playfully punches his arm laughing making him start laughing along with her.

****

INSIDE THE HOTEL LUMP AND KEISHA

"Eww shit, fuck me NIGGA!" Shouts Keisha who's on her knees while Lump hits her from the back. The loud smacking of their skins colliding with each other fills the room. "Take all this dick! I'mma fuck the shit out of you!" shouted Lump.

"Damn... your dick...feel good... make meee cum!" Backing her ass up against Lump, Keisha begins playing with her clit between her legs. Every time they're bodies collide together Keisha's titties bounce forward. Her body begins to orgasm, Lump begins to cum, and collapses on top of her.

"Hell yeah you can get it again! You... DID NOT disappoint!" said Keisha.
"Your pussy good as shit Keisha. You got a nigga sweating and shit. Damn!"
They both begin laughing.

****

NEXT ROOM OVER
MELVO AND BREE

"You moving way too fast... slooo... slow down." said Bree while in her head she's thinking, "Damn, what the fuck..." Melvo is saying to himself, "Nigga, don't cum too fast."

"Thaaaats it, that's it, right there slow down...eww yeah...that's it... keep it, right there..." What, the fuck! Nigga, I know you ain't cum already... I don't believe this shit you got cum all on my leg!" yelled Bree. "My bad... I---- "Melvo

41

slowly to speak embarrassed he began looking down.

"You ain't never did this before?" asked Bree.
"Nawl…" Melvo looked up with a half-smile.
"Why you ain't say something?"
"I'm supposed to just tell you?"
"Look, I'm here because I like you, you got potential… Let's start again. Put your hands on my titties… Yeah... take your time, yeah, that's it…nice and slow…

****

ALLANTE' AND HEATHER'S ROOM

Allante' is laying on the bed butt naked when Heather walks out of the bathroom naked. He sits up straight while watching her walk over to the bed. Heather crawls up on to him, and stands up over him with her pussy in his face, she looks down at his hard dick squatting herself down until his dick disappears inside of her. Sitting on top of him now face to face, she looks deeply into his eyes, placing her arms around his neck, he kisses her lips, and then puts her right nipple inside of his mouth.
She begins to rock back and forth around and around, moaning out loudly in pleasure as their tempo heats up.

Their sex can be heard as his dick goes in and out of her. He places his arm around her waist, as she bounces up and down calling his name. "Allante', I love you... Fuck me please, fuck me...." They heated up, Allante' rolls her over onto her back pushing her legs back, he long dicks her and all she does is moan out louder.

Pulling out of her, he turns her over, and places a pillow under her, entering her from behind. "You... you the maaaa man daddy, be beat it up!" stuttered Heather. Allante' takes his que, and starts to pull out as far as he can, only leaving the head of his dick in, and throwing his body into her. His pelvic bone can be heard slapping up against her ass every time, and with every stroke

Heather moans louder and louder. "Shit! What you doing!"
"Take this dick!"
"Beee-- beat it up then!" Allante' pumps harder and faster and Heather is softly screaming in pleasure. "I'm cu--- cumming Alla!" Allante' shoots his cum inside of her while she cums all over his dick. Laying on top of her, she is still squeezing her pussy muscles on his dick draining all of his cum out of him inside of her. They soon fall asleep with him laying halfway on top of her. Heather is deeply in love.

SCENE 2:
ROAMING IN THE THICK BRUSH

BACK IN DETROIT
THE PHONE RINGS

"Fool, this nigga just disrespected me!" said Lump. "Where you at?" answered Allante'. "I'm at Dot and Etta's off Livernois."
"I'm on my way." Several minutes later, Allante' calls Lump back. "Hello?"
"What he got on?"
"He outside with some jean shorts on and a blue Polo. It's about five of them-

Boom!!! The sound of a loud gun going off erupts over the phone line. "Oh shit!" said Lump ducking down. Outside people are scattering while one body is laying on the ground and a black male with a black hoodie on is seen running away. A young black male has been shot in the leg, but he will survive...

ALLANTE' HOUSE
1642 MONICA STREET

"Fool, when you bust that heat, I ain't know what was happening I thought them niggas was busting at me. How you get around there so fast?"
"I ran nigga! I ain't know what was happening so I ain't play with it."

"Did anybody see your face?" asked Melvo. "I had the hoodie on... it was a little girl on one of the porches, she was about eleven or twelve, but she ain't see my face... it could've been somebody looking out of a window, I don't know...Lump did you know them niggas?" asked Allante' "I seen them around the way over on Fenkell before, but I don't know them..."

"Look, lay low, and don't go out by yourself. We got to find out where they from."
"Bet." said Lump. "How we gone do that fool?" asked Melvo. "Niggas love to talk, and so do broads. All we gotta do is be quiet and listen. The streets do more telling than anybody. Niggas always out there talking about what they not suppose to...trust me we'll find them just give it a couple of days...just watch." ended Allante'.

****

THREE DAYS LATER

Lump did you hear about that boy who got shot by Dot & Etta's?" Keisha asked Lump. "When?" asked Lump. "Three days ago, boy! That shit happened right over there where y'all live at, and you don't know about it?"
"Nawl."
"Um hmm, well, the boy's name is Nate, he got two brothers and it's about four other boys he hang with

they stay on Cherrylawn between Puritan and 6 Mile."
"Why you tellin' me?"
"I just thought you should know, I heard they think somebody around y'all way shot him, be careful."

"We good, we ain't have nothing to do with that, but good looking out."
"When I'm gon get some dick?"
"Shit you can get this dick whenever you want it."
"Um hmm, I need it to be hard."
"As a rock!"
"Sneak in my window tonight."
"You a freak azz bitch."
"You love it."
"Leave the window unlocked."

LUMP AND MELVO HOUSE

"Fool, you ain't lie, Keisha called me and said the nigga name Nate and he got two brothers and it's about four other dudes in their crew and they live on Cherrylawn." Nodding his head. "That means we'll definitely see them again but it's too close." said Melvo. "Don't trip, I'mma make it loud and clear, that they don't want no work with us."
"I'm going with you Alla." said Lump. "Me too nigga! Whatever you do we doing it together."

"Aiight, we got to find where they live and where they hang out and then we gon put our lick down, remember we always do shit to get away."

"Fool, where you learn that?" asked Lump. "I just be thinking shit Slim…it just come to me."

****

Allante's cell phone begins ringing. "What's up beautiful?"
"I need to talk to you it's important." said Heather with a serious voice. "Aiight I'm on my way." Allante' ended the call. Allante' turns to the brothers. "Slim, I got to go y'all. I'm going over to Heather's call me if something comes up."
"Bet." Both of the brothers respond in unison.

****

AT HEATHER'S HOUSE

"Hello, Ms. Brown." Smiled Allante' as he entered the doorway. "Hey baby, go ahead to Heather's room. She's up there."
"Thank you." Allante' leaned in kissing Heather's mother on her cheek. Walking up the steps he enters Heather's bedroom seeing Josh playing on the floor, Josh looks up seeing Allante' he lights up. Allante' picks him up sitting down with him on Heather's bed where Heather is sitting talking on the phone.

"Okay Heffa, I'll call you later." Heather ended her phone call, looking at Allante'. "I know you had something to do with that boy getting shot." said Heather matter-of-factly.

"What you mean?"

"Allante' that's yo neighborhood. YOUR NEIGHBORHOOD, don't nothing happen around there without, you, Lump, and Melvo not knowing about it, and giving the okay."

"Heather------- she quickly cut him off.
"Look at me, I know you Allante', I study you and you make my heart beat so PLEASE don't lie to me. You know I would never betray you just look at how you take care of me and my son and above everything else I love you Allante'."

"Heather, you blowing this shit way out of proportion." Allante' jumped up from his seat.
"No, I'm not… I don't ever want to lose you…and those dudes are looking for the boy they got into it with at Dot & Etta's and the person who shot him, and the police are looking for them also."
"Look at me Heather, I'mma handle this."
"What you about to do? You gon kill'em all?"
"If they make me."

"What about your future, what about your mother, your brothers, and what about me and Josh?" her mouth trembled with every word spoken.
"Heather, them niggas ain't even laying like that!"
"It's not about them, it's about the chances you are taking…you have a future Allante' and I'm tied in it… can't you see I'm connected to you."

"Heather, look at me, I'm not gone ever let a threat stay around."

"Well what do you need me to do?"

"What do you mean?"

"I'm a part of you... your problem is my problem, I can find out where they live and where they be at." She then added, "Keisha already on it."

"Look-----

"Nawl look shit, I'mma always have your back cause I belong to you... What we gone do with our lives Alla?"

"Our whole life is ahead of us Heather."

"But we have to have a plan, you always say that."

"I have a plan Heather."

"What is it Allante'?"

"Beautiful, I got money and a lot of it... I just can't do nothing with it right now, because I'm too young to own my own shit. Buying it, would bring a tip to myself. I got enough money to buy you a house, cars, and whatever else we want."

"Allante' you're smart azz shit and sometimes I be like, is he really sixteen years old because you're on a level that these grown men ain't on out here. Make me understand why you think the way you do?"

"My father had another son, his name is Antonio and he's in heaven." Allante' lowered his head then looked back up into Heather's eyes. "He got shot and killed by a police UNARMED in what they claim was an attempted robbery but they ain't never find no gun."

Shit black boys and men be gettin gunned down by white people especially the fucking police and don't shit happen." Tears are welling up inside of Heather's eyes. "Police think they Gods... they supposed to serve and protect...yeah right...they just shoot to kill." Allante' angrily spoke through his clenched teeth, "I be wanting to kill every white police I see and every black police that protect what them white bitches do just to be a part of the force."

He calmed his demeanor just before looking into directly at Heather and said, "Look...like this drug shit, I mean I know its wrong Heather but the money helps me do what I want to do. I see these bitch azz niggas out here who got bread and don't help nobody so I take their shit. I see these weak azz niggas out here and I be wanting to kill up all these niggas... especially the older ones. It's a whole lost generation of black kids out here, and these niggas don't give a fuck about us... I didn't make Josh, but I love him like he's mines. You don't have to make a child to love him and help him grow.

All these fake azz rappers, basketball players, football and baseball players, I don't want to be like them. I want to be much better and preachers are weak too, from what I know about Jesus, he stood up for the poor, women, children and old people. All this shit is fucked up Heather, and even as young as I am, I can see all of it…"

"Go see your father." said Heather. "They won't let me in by myself; I'm too young to go alone so my mother has to take me."
"So why won't you ask her to take you…?"
"I'll think about it." Allante' laid back on the bed with Josh sleep on his chest soon after. Heather laid down right beside him. With her left arm wrapped around him and Josh.

****

3 DAYS LATER
ALLANTE' HOUSE

"Ma, I want to go see my father…" After a moment of silence, his mother responded, "For what Allante'?" Trying his best to act nonchalant.
"It's just questions that keep running through my mind and stuff I need to say to him, and things I need answers too, it's not about you Ma… it's about me…"
"I'll take you up there."
"I want to go this weekend… you can just go up there then get me in and leave. You can go shopping and I'll call you after the visit is over for you to come and pick me up… okay Ma?"
"Oh yeah?"

"Out of all the women in the world, God chose you to give me life and I thank you…you know you my first love." Allante' said smiling.

"You were a very smart baby Allante', and you've grown to be a handsome young man, your brothers love you, and they look up to you as well and I love you too and I'm so proud of you."

****

JACKSON PENITENTIARY
JACKSON, MICHIGAN

"Light you have a visit!" announce the correctional officer.

"Alright, I'll be ready in about five minutes." responded Antonio Light sitting up on his bunk to prepare to go out to the visitation floor.

****

VISITING ROOM

Deborah Light, and Allante' are sitting at a visiting table when Allante's father walks up.

"Hello Deborah."

"Hello Tony."

"You're still as beautiful as the day I met you."

She smiled responding, "And you're still as handsome at the first day I met you…well I just came in to get your son in cause he wants to talk to you alone; Allante' call me when you're ready."

"Alright Ma, I love you." She leaves the father and son sitting across from one another.

"You look just like me when I was your age and when you were younger I called you my mini-me. Making you son... I know I did something right." "I remember you and I love you so much Dad..." "I had you walking at seven months Allante' and your first word was Daddy... you said that before you said Mama; son you were a beautiful baby."

He beamed with pride as he continued on, "You know when you came into this world, you didn't even cry. I was there in the delivery room man your eyes were wide open and you were just looking around the room. You were and are a special child, so what brings you here?"

Looking confused Allante asked, "So tell me why did you stop communicating with me?"
"It has bothered me my whole life Dad and I felt like you just stop loving me and caring about me and as much as I love you I've been angry at you... you left me... you just left me..."

"Alla, when your mother had you, I was young and at fourteen I already had your brother Antonio ... man I was growing up fast."
"Your mother lived two doors down from me and she was a virgin, in fact the first time your mother and I had sex she got pregnant."

Did you know she was only fifteen when she got pregnant with you, and sixteen when she had you?" "I was still boxing and going to school and then you came into the world and for the first year of your life me and your mother were together."

I wanted to give y'all a better life, so I started small time hustling but it wasn't enough." Tony continued, "Next I went into the streets and it led to selling drugs, robbing jewelry stores and banks then a dude told on me and everything started to crumble."

"The police threatened your mother because they didn't know exactly who I was but because of the informant they knew she was close to me." "She didn't give them any information on me when they questioned her at the house but once they took her downtown to question her I went and I turned myself in. I told them it was me that they was looking for so they would let her go." I just didn't want her to go through that so I took my weight son… It's consequences to the street Allante'."

"So why you and my mother ain't together?" "I'd rather her live her life, than be locked up with me cause that'd been selfish so I told her to go ahead and live her life." Tony spoke firmly, "Look at me, it was never my intentions for your mother to have to raise you by herself."

"When I held you for the first time and you looked up at me while I knew I loved your mother no love in the world could compare itself like seeing myself when I looked at you."

"I send her money home from here, what else could I do?" Tony searched his son's face for an answer. "I realized that I didn't stop having responsibilities because I got locked up so I told her to live her life Allante' but she still wanted to be with me and I pushed her away."
"But why?"
"Again, it would be selfish of me to expect her to not have sex, not go out and have fun, and not get help taking care of you; love is not selfish."

"She met somebody and had two more kids but the dude was a sucker; look whenever I tell your mother to come see me she does and she sends me money without me having to ask her. We've looked out for one another all these years because we are friends and that's all I can ask for and give is loyalty."

"But that ain't telling me why you don't communicate with me though?" Allante' asked in a more frustrated tone. "I looked at where I am and didn't I think that I was the best example for you to follow."
"Dad I needed to hear from you."
"Alla, listen to me son... you are me!

"Man at sixteen years old you are way more gifted and mature than most males will ever get to be in their whole lifetime and you've just begun." "You've already done more than I ever got a chance to do when I was on the streets."

"I've learned so much more about me and now I can teach you how to be more than me. I don't want you to be like me I want you to be better than me."
"I got a problem."
"It can be solved..." Tony said with assurety..." talk, I'm listening."

"I hit a couple licks out here and I don't know how to get rid of the stuff I got."
"Tell me what you did?"
"The first thing me and two boys went up in this house, got some weed, a brick and some money, it was a broad and dude up in the house, the broad lived but the dude had to go."
Then we caught another major lick... we caught a Mexican stash house.
Dad, we got eighty bricks, and a few million dollars, I had to wet three Mexicans." His father frowned,
"Did y'all clean up good behind yourself?"
"Dad we always wear gloves and ski masks. In all them kills I used a knife and I never use the same one all the knives are different. I get rid of the blades and the clothes and we ain't never leaving no

D.N.A....plus we do all of the work in the a.m. so being seen by a bystander is slim to none... but here's the thing... we ain't trying to sell no drugs we just trying to get money.

We ain't bought no cars or anything like that, we just be buying clothes and we waiting cause we got plans...big plans for like all of the businesses we want to start but we know we can't explain the money right now...so how do we get rid of the coke?"

"Listen up, I got a friend who just got out and he like a big brother to me; his name is Terrance Williams, but they call him T out there. He lives on the eastside and when he was out there he was a big boy. He got caught with five Ki's of raw and a million dollars cash. He put a lot of niggas on in Detroit when he was out there. I'mma give you his number. I talk to him about you all the time and he's my family so you're like his nephew, you can trust him like you trust me so listen to him and you'll never have to sell no drugs..."
"I'mma call him when I get back, and me and my boys will go see him".
"What's your boys' name?"
"Lump and Melvo."

"Hey, I got two Western Union money transfers for $5,000.00 dollars apiece in the name of Brown. Did you send that?"

"I had my girl send it to you… we good out here dad trust me we eatin'. Aye Dad listen my mother don't know nothing about this."

"And she'll never hear it from me…you got anything else?"

"I got a couple of niggas out here that I might have to deal with but they ain't ready for the work I put in." Leaning forward in a stern tone Tony said, "Always plan to get away." Antonio then continued, "Alla, I could tell you don't do this and do that but then you wouldn't tell me anything. It's not what I want you to do, but if you're going to do it son I'mma make sure you get away with it. Just know that his can't be your life and this lifestyle don't last long." Allante' stood up from the table, and he looks his dad in the eyes. "Dad, I'm already rich, I just can't show it yet…."

IN THE CAR DRIVING BACK TO DETROIT

"Sooooo how did it go?" asked Deborah. "I learned a lot and you been going to see my dad all this time huh and in my heart I couldn't understand why he ain't been a part of my life."

"Your father pushed me away. It was times when I drove up there and he refused my visits. And no, I'm not going to make a man accept me but I understand why he did it. Allante he had to focus on where he's at and how to get through that his way but my sole responsibility was taking care of you and I don't make no apology for the decisions I've made."

"That's not---- his mother cut back in over him. "Let me finish I had you at sixteen and although I loved him he made choices and I still loved him unconditionally after those choices were made; he told me to be happy and I'm doing the best I can."

"But you ain't happy Ma… I hear you in the room crying when you got the door closed… I know you not happy cause you let that weak nigga come into our life and you knew I didn't like him."
"Why Allante'… why didn't you like him?"
"Man cause he hit you!" Allante yelled at his mother.

Looking over at her son in shock because he'd never dare to disrespect her in any way but she could see the pain in his eyes. Allante's face showed her a look of apology but those exact words never came from his mouth instead he continued, "Do you know how I felt at ten years old standing in front of a grown man telling him you not going to hit my mother…."

"I was scared to death… how could I ever love a nigga who hit my momma?" Allante' threw his hands up in the air, "To top it off then and you asked me if you married him would I take his last name?" Shaking his head Allante sighed a deep breathe, "My last name is Light...after my father, he's RJ and Andre's father and I'm glad that niggas gone cause I wanted to kill him."

Allante' continued, "I used to think you didn't love me... do you know what it feels like for a kid when he think his mother the ONE person in the world who supposed to love him don't love him... mannnn it hurt. I love both of my brothers but I'm glad you're not with their father.

I don't understand why you ever were to be honest Ma cause you're beautiful. You ain't never gotta chase a man. You go to work, come home cook for us and then go to your room and close the door... you don't even know me Ma."

"Do you think I don't see the clothes you wear but I can tell you that I know what I bought you and what I didn't." She looked at him with a side-eye... "I don't know exactly what you're doing and I don't want my heart broke so I don't ask." Allante' turned his head to face the window but that didn't stop his mother because now it was her turn to let off some steam... "I come to your fights and watched you score among the top ten in the state on your SAT scores, you are my first born and I love you… no I'm not perfect …his mother shook her head and let out a half laugh but I do my best."

"I know I made mistakes but I provide for you and your brothers the best I can. I put the best clothes on you that money can buy and you live in a house that is mines and you've never known hunger or poverty and those are the things that make me happy Allante' NOT a man"
"I love you mama."
"And I love you too Allante'."
He kisses his mother on the cheek and she drove on up the highway content.

LATER THAT NIGHT
ALLANTE' HOUSE

Melvo, Lump and Allante' are in the basement playing the Play Station.
"We got a meeting in two days about getting rid of those bricks." said Allante' "How you work that out?" asked Melvo. "I went to see my father today."
"You went up Jackson?" asked Lump
"Yeah Mo, you wouldn't believe the shit I heard today."
"What's up?" Asked Melvo
"My mother been going up there off and on for years to see my father."
"Mane get the fuck outta here. Mrs. Light?"
"Man, she don't go nowhere" said Lump. "I been mad at this nigga cause I thought he said fuck me I couldn't understand it."

"So, where y'all at now?" asked Melvo.
"We good… I told him about the lick and he gave me his man number, and said his man would move it for us and then give us the money. I told him we rob drug dealers but we don't sell drugs."
"Bet, so what's up?" asked Lump.

"I called the dude, his name is T and he supposed to be laying like that. Him and my father like brothers and he just got out a few months ago before he went upstate my father said he used to be that guy. My father had already talked to him and told him about me and to expect my call. He told us to come see him on Monday; he lounging on the eastside…I think he said on Dequindre by East 6 Mile. If he talking good like I hope he is we can get rid of that shit ASAP so we ain't going to school that day."

"Cool, it's on." said Lump. "Did y'all hear anything else on those niggas?" asked Allante'. "Keisha told me they be hanging at the Blue Room Lounge off of Fenkell and Wyoming.

Them niggas like twenty-one and twenty-two years old; she said they stay on Cherrylawn and Roselawn." said Lump. "How many of them is it all together?" asked Allante'. "It's bout seven of them… the dude Nate got two brothers and his four friends." said Melvo. "Well, I don't give a fuck how many of them it is cause if they want some work

I'mma burn they asses up. I ain't gon never wait for a nigga to come to us." ended Allante". "They say them niggas be at that spot every night so it's sweet."

"The parking lot is located directly in front of the club across the street and it's almost on the corner of a street with houses. They say the backdoor of the joint be wide open." He paused before continuing trying to recollect all of the info he got on the layout. "It's a bar on the left when you come in the door but the dance floor is on the right, and the pool table is towards the back." Allante' began, "I got something for they asses!"
"Bet." responded the brothers in unison.

****

TUESDAY 10:30 a.m.
INSIDE T'S HOUSE

"What's up man, I'm Allante'. This is Lump and Melvo." Shaking hands, they all entered the house. "What's up." said Lump and Melvo.
"You look just like your father; have a seat." said T. They all sat down and T began, "So talk to me." Without hesitation Allante' got straight to the point, "We got some birds we trying to get rid of and my father told me to come holler at you so what can you do for us?" T tried to hide his excitement "Oh yeah how much y'all talking bout?" asked T. "We got a few." said Lump. "Mr. Light said you laying like that." said Melvo. "Well young bull… T rubbed

the top of his head…I used to be but for now let's just say I know people. Your father is my little brother so you my family and y'all his men so y'all my family too."

"Bet!" said all three friends in unison.

"I can move however much y'all got. What y'all want for it?"

"We want---"$15 stacks a brick." Allante' cut Melvo off. Lump and Melvo look at Alla. Allante' continues, "What type of weight are you or your people moving?"

"Allante', I don't move nothing, I have people moving for me simply on the strength of who I am; so, whatever you got it don't compare to what goes through my hands." T said with a half-smile.

"We ain't drug dealers Mo, we just came up on a lick." said Allante'.

"Fifteen a brick is cool… whatever y'all got, I'll take it."

"Cool, we'll holler at you tomorrow. We out." said Allante', and the three youngsters stood up leaving.

****

IN THE CUTLASS

"Why only fifteen fool?" asked Melvo. "We not drug dealers Slim so we put it at a price a nigga can't refuse. We ain't pay for it so it's all profit for us…. Do you even know how much that is? Fifteen thousand times eighty is $1,200,000.00 dollars... That's $400,000.00 dollars apiece. We already millionaires Mo." finished Allante'. "I ain't never think of it like that. Damn, you right." said Melvo happily.

"Mo, I swear we blessed cause we only sixteen years old and we rich." Allante' smiled.
"Melvo now you can go to design school and cause you already got the money to start your clothing line while you are actually in school learning to be a designer and Lump you can start going to the auction and buying cars to flip them and wash your money.

We ain't gon be like everybody else I'm telling y'all our whole hood gone be eating. First, we got to see these niggas, my fingers are itching." Lump cut in, "Nigga, you crazy!"
"Wait till after you bust a nigga and then tell me how you feel." said Allante'. "Let's work." said Melvo.

A FEW NIGHTS LATER
12 a.m.

Across the street from the Blue Room Lounge in the parking lot the crew sits inside of Allante's Cutlass. "You see that nigga with the crutches?" asked Melvo; pointing across the street, "That's Nate... there they go."
"Man, this shit sweet, them niggas ain't got a clue. Fool we on some Lions in the jungle laying in the

grass shit." said Lump. Melvo then said, "Nigga, Lions ain't in the jungle, that's Tigers."
"You know what I'm saying nigga." said Lump.
"So how y'all wanna do it?" asked Allante'.

"It's a couple of ways we can do it mane… I'mma get us a car we can put it in two streets back so it's away from the noise. Matter of fact I'mma get two cars and we'll sit in one here in the parking lot that I'll have it already here in the parking lot. Let me come a couple more nights and make sure these niggas like clockwork." ended Melvo.

"This your play Mo, we ready when you say go." responded Allante'. "Alla you thought more about what T said?" asked Lump. "Yeah. I think we should give him twenty joints at a time, what y'all think?" Melvo shrugged, "If he can move like you say he can then it should only take a couple of weeks. I like him and we could use a old head. He might be able to help us on some other shit too." said Melvo.

"Aye Slim, I saw this house on W. Outer Drive off of 6 Mile and I want us to get that joint."
"We need our own spot. We got like $250,000.00 in the pot. Get that joint." said Melvo. "I'mma work on it." said Allante'. "I'm bout to buy me a car." said Lump. "What you gon get?" asked Allante
"I'mma surprise y'all."
"Do you Mo, you got it."

"Let's get outta here bro cause I'm trying to some pussy I'm bout to go over Bree's house." said Melvo. "Aye fool drop me off over Keisha's house!" said Lump smiling. "Aiight, Heather already over my house Mo cause my mother love the shit out of her!"

"Slim, I ain't gon lie you and Shorty fit together, for real mane y'all look good together." "She laying like that but you know I was going to book her first." said Melvo. "Get the fuck outta here." Said Allante' and Lump at the same time laughing.

7 a.m.
NEXT DAY
ALLANTE'S HOUSE

"Wake up Allante', you gon be late." said Heather getting dressed. "Man, I'm tired azz shit." "I got to drop Josh off at Sleepy Hollow and I can't be late for that or school so get up!" Rubbing his eyes "Aiight man, shit."
"Boy don't make me late."
"I got you Bae."

****

IN THE CUTLASS

"How is the hair school coming along?" asked Allante' driving down the street. "It's called

Cosmetology school and we learn how to do hair, nails, toes, feet, and we even learn about make-up."

"You don't need no makeup, you got beautiful skin."
"Thank you, babe."
"For what?"
"You just naturally say things that lift me up.
You the shit daddy; hey guess what…I think I got a name for my first shop I'mma call it, "Another Level!"
"Cause you gone take it to another level."
"You got that right."
"You can do it Shorty, you can do whatever you put your mind too."

Heather leans in kissing Allante' on his cheeks.
"I love you."
"I love you too."

****

LATER IN ALLANTE' CAR
HIS CELL PHONE RINGS

"Hello?" said Allante, he hears a clicking sound, "You have a pre-paid call from Antonio Light, an inmate at a correctional facility hang up to deny the call, or press five to accept-
Allante' immediately pressed five.
"What's up Pops?"

"Hey son, how are you?"
"I'm cool, bout to go to the gym cause I got a fight next week."
"You ready?"

"Dad, I can't explain it but it's crazy cause I don't even have to think to do it stuff just comes and I see everything." Feeling proud Tony told his son, "You got a gift, I use to make you imitate me. You used to throw your little punches. It's in you."
"We hollered at that dude, we good." said Allante'.
"He's family so what else is up with you?"
"I want to get some houses and some commercial property downtown."
"T is hip to all that plus he got a lot of houses around the city so he can help you out on that too."

"When you getting out dad?"
"I got like sixteen months left." Antonio sighed.
I'mma trying to see how much half-way house time I could get. If I can get a year, I'll be out in six months, if not, in nine months to a year."
"What you gone do when you get out here?"
"I got a plan, we'll talk about it when you come see me again."
"Alright."

"So, what's up with this lil girl you got? Your mother told me you got a little cutie."
"She's my heart, her name is Heather and she has a little son name Josh; that's my lil man."

"How you feel about her?"

"I know she love me Dad plus her mother let me stay over her crib and Ma let her stay over."

"So, you really into her?"

"Wait until you see her!"

"Alright, bring her up here."

"Alright, bet."

Allante's phone beeps.

"Look this fifteen minute collect phone call about to cut off."

"Aiight Pop, call me anytime do you need something?"

"No, I'm good son, be careful out there."

"Aiight Dad, I love you."

"I love you too son."

****

KRONKS BOXING GYM

"That's right, move son! Head movement! Keep your hands up! Move...move now side to side, in and out! Jab... one...one... two...jab! Go to the head body now work!" coached Mr. Logan.

"Mr. Logan, I'm trying to turn pro."

"Allante', your good enough son you're just not old enough yet, when you get seventeen we can definitely go and take the steps to see about how to turn you Pro. and from there you'll have a title in a year!" The look of frustration was all over his face.

70

"That seems so far away." Equally bummed "Allante', son listen to me… you got the talent just be patient."

Don't rush cause when people rush that's when they make mistakes. You got a couple of months until you turn seventeen, then we'll go from there." His coach and mentor patted him on the shoulder. "Aiight coach." Allante' nodded in agreement. "Go ahead, and get dressed, good work, I'll see you tomorrow.

****

ALLANTE' SITTING INSIDE OF CAR
IN FRONT OF HEATHER'S HOUSE

The cellular phone rings…
"Hello?"
"Come outside."
"Alright Bae."
Heather opens the front door seeing Allante' sitting in a champagne colored Nissan Maxima.
"Whose car is this?"
"It's yours!"
Heather screams, "Ahhhh! I can't believe it!" She begins fanning herself with her hands while tears fall down her face from her eyes. "Hold up, what you crying for?"
"You bought this for me?"
"Yeah."

Heather begins inspecting the car noticing that on the backseat there is a car seat. "Now you can stop waking me up and you can drive yourself where you need to go." Allante' laughed. Standing side by side, Heather turns placing her arm around his neck and starts kissing him all over his face before placing her soft lips on his.

"Thank you." said Heather sincerely when they pull apart. "We got to get you some car insurance." Heather pulls her cell phone out to call Keisha. "Bitch I got a car... who you think bought it bitch? ... It's a Maxima…." Jumping up and down Heather shouts, "BITCH I GOT A CAR!"

****

ALLANTE' AT THE STOPLIGHT

A car pulls alongside Allante'. The driver side window of the car next to him rolls down. Allante' looking over into the car smiles. "Nigga you in that shit!" said Allante'. Melvo smiles back at him cause he's driving his 760 smoke grey B.M.W., "I couldn't help it fool! This motherfucker was calling me!" "That joint fit you, that joint fit you like shit!" Melvo is wearing a wide smile as he speaks, "Alla, the nigga fixed the paper work so I'm only paying $400.00 dollars a month, meet me at my house." Waving his hand out of the window; "Bet!" They skirt off into traffic. "Man, this motherfucker laying like that! Nigga you make me want to go get some shit!" said Allante', getting out of his vehicle in front of Melvo's house.

Lump pulls up in a shiny platinum colored S550 Mercedes Benz with pure cocaine white interior. "What the fuck!" exclaimed Allante' now looking at Lump getting out of his new car to join him and Melvo at the curb. "Yeah nigga this bitch ain't playing!" said Lump smiling. "Yeah Slim, this bitch mean, y'all gone make me get on some serious shit, both these motherfuckers mean." Gathered around their new toys; "We young paid niggas fool!" said Lump, then he added, "I'mma drive this motherfucker!" The three best friends all smiled.

****

HEATHER, KEISHA, AND BREE
THREE-WAY PHONE CALL

"Bitch did you see them cars!? Them niggas getting it. Shit I ain't know that when we met them niggas in the mall shit was gon turn out like this." said Keisha. "All three of them niggas got it. I'mma make this pussy talk to that nigga, next time he fuck me." said Bree. They all laughed. "We got to hold them down." said Keisha "Bitch I'm holding mines down. It don't matter what he got or what he don't got all I know is he got me." said Heather. "They gon make it happen but they so young so how they get it like that?" Said Bree. "They had it before they met us so it don't even matter bitch... don't be nosey, be happy." said Heather aggressively. "True, bitch I'm happy ass shit and his dick good." said Keisha. "Bitch you crazy." said Heather. "Shit, I taught my nigga how to fuck so he gon pay me for my lessons." said Bree bragging. "Whore" replied Heather and Keisha in unison. The three friends burst into a fit of laughter.

****

SCENE 3:
IT'S FEEDING TIME...

12:30 a.m.
BLUE ROOM LOUNGE PARKING LOT

Melvo is sitting in his car talking into his cell phone speaker. "Fool, they on clock-work, every night, same time." said Melvo. "Aiight, let's get them niggas tomorrow low-key niggas say they been riding through our way but they just don't know who we are... stupid azz niggas, I'll holler at you tomorrow." finished Allante'. "Bet!" Melvo ended the call.

THE NEXT NIGHT 11 P.M.
BLUE ROOM LOUNGE PARKING LOT

Sitting inside of a money green Chrysler mini-van Melvo, Lump and Allante' wait for their victims.
"When we see them and we get out I'mma come from the front then Lump you come from straight across the street but walk in the middle just know they gone see you first then Alla you come from the back." said Melvo "Mo these Glock .40's is sweet azz shit!" said Allante'. "I got us a gun connect." said Melvo. "Yeah, I need about five of these." said Allante'. Leaning across the front seat of the car; "Alla, when you gone get a whip?" asked Lump. "Y'all niggas got me thinking... I got something in mind... oh trust me it's coming..." he smiled.

1 HOUR LATER

"There they go, let's move." said Melvo. Just then Melvo eases the driver side door open bending down he starts ducking up and down while running posting behind cars in the parking lot. Toward the left he crouches down behind one cars bumper. Allante' runs in the other direction to get in position behind the prey. Lump is waiting by the van standing behind the passenger side front bumper while their victims don't have a clue what's about to happen.

The group of vics are walking and talking towards the club, never noticing the three shadows moving across the street. The vics look up, and suddenly it's too late… The vics all reach for their waist line and before they can grab their weapons sparks begin to fly. The defending sounds of the guns booming successively followed by bodies dropping, and screams of horror erupt. Dressed in all black with their ski-masks down over their faces Melvo, Lump and Allante' run up on the falling bodies. Standing over them, Melvo point his gun at Nate's face.

"This your fault nigga!" BOOM!!!
The gun jerks back in Melvo's hand next thing he knows he's watching the back of Nat's head explode. "Please I don't want this!" pleaded one of the vics. "Bitch shut up!" said Lump. BOOM!!!

Two are now dead for sure, the other victim tries to crawl away, and Allante' points his gun aiming it at the back of his ass he starts shooting, hitting him with one bullet in his ass and in the back of his head dropping him. "Let's go!" announced Lump.

The young three lions run back across the street cutting through the parking lot, then hopping through someone's backyard, sprinting across another street and through more backyards to where their get-away car is parked.

In the second mini-van that has tinted windows the three of them take off their ski-mask, Melvo drives away. "AYE! Y'all good!" asked Melvo. "We good Mo, just drive calm." said Allante'. "We gone throw these guns off the bridge at Belle Isle and we can leave this shit there too cause my car down there already." said Melvo.
"Alla, I love you fool, you already know since we were nine." said Melvo sincerely.

"Nigga, I met him first, I met you at the corner store playing Mrs. Pac Man." said Lump. "I know y'all niggas ain't bout to get into that shit again." said Allante'. "Nawl, I just mean you always there with me and him; remember we all used to sleep piled up in the same bed… it's just like you came out of our mother's womb too, we love you fool!" said Melvo. "I love y'all two...too, Aye Mo, don't be getting all mushy on me." Lump smiled looking at Allante', "Mane fuck you."

****

NEXT DAY
10 A.M. NEWS

"Three dead, two critical and two in fair condition. Next on Eye Witness News... "Hello, I'm Tina Dance, reporting live here at the Blue Room Lounge on Fenkell where at about 12:30 last night a barrage of gun fire left three young men dead, two in critical condition and two in fair condition; while it's not clear what led to this heinous shooting in the past two months there have been multiple killings in this area. Residents and City officials alike are calling for police to provide answer and suspects." I'm Tina Dance reporting live this is Detroit eye Witness News."

DETROIT, MI, HOMICIDE, ROBBERY DIVISON
CAPTIN JACKSON

"Campbell, what the hell is going on over there between Fenkell and Puritan?" We've had a total of four homicides, then a shooting at Dot and Etta's, and now another triple homicide with two more in critical condition." said Captain Jackson.

"Captain, Brooks and I haven't got any leads so far from the citizens that we've interviewed." He slowly turned in her direction. "What the hell you mean no leads?" A defeated Campbell spoke up, "Nobody in the community seemed to see anything. All of the crimes are happening in the early morning hours, there's no finger-prints and no D.N.A. left behind. Whoever this is they are cleaning up after themselves very well."

He slammed his hands on her desk and foamed at the mouth as he spoke, "I got the Mayor and the Chief of Police up my ass! If you can't handle this shit, I'll find somebody who can!" Campbell looked both worried and frustrated. "Captain I'm doing the best I can.", trying her best not to sound unnerved. "I don't want to hear that shit! And neither does the families of these victims, the Chief, or the goddamn Mayor, get some results." Captain Jackson leaves her.

"Man, he's mad ass shit." said Brooks. Campbell gives Brooks a hard-cold stare. "No shit, I thought I told you to go over to Sinai/Grace Hospital, and talk to the surviving witness?" "I did Bernice." She starred at him intensely. "And?" Brooks then shrugged his shoulders nonchalantly, "All black clothes, ski-masks in fact they both said they didn't see them until they were already up on them. Other than that, they're not talking." "Well, do you think they know who did this?" "If they don't, they're sitting ducks."

"Did they say how many they saw?"

"Yeah they said it was three."

"Three?"

"Yeah, three and we collected a lot of shell cases from .40 Cal weapons and we got a few slugs so ballistics is checking them now."

"That witness on the Lilac triple homicide said they saw three people leaving the house, but those murders were done with a knife hmmmph she placed her hands on her hips debating thoughts in her head… I'm not sure. Listen, the two guys in fair condition both had guns on them. If they don't cooperate, threaten to charge them with possession of a firearm…maybe that will get them to talk."

HIGH SCHOOL PARKING LOT
MUSIC PLAYING IN LUMP'S S550

"Fool that shit was all on the news this morning!" said Lump. "Two in critical, two fair and three dead. We need to get them niggas." said Allante'. "They at Sinai/Grace." said Melvo. "Ain't no mercy Dawg they gotta go." said Allante'. "I got an idea on how we can get them." said Lump.

****

8 p.m.
SINAI/GRACE HOSPITAL 2ND FLOOR

Two black males with janitorial uniforms on are walking down the 2nd floor hallway pushing mop buckets. As they get to room 203, they reach into the mop buckets and pull out two nail gnus. The two janitors walk quietly into the room while the two young men are sleeping in their beds unaware that death just walked into the room.

"Phm Phm Phm Phm Phm Phm." The nails from the nail gun silently enter the faces and heads of Clarence Thomas, twenty-two, and Alfonso Bryant, twenty-three instantly ending their lives, the two young men never wake up again. The janitors walk calmly out of the room pushing their mop buckets turning to walk down the steps and out of the front lobby never to be seen again.

Outside in the parking lot of the hospital Allante' waits for his best friends as they walk up to the stolen mini-van where he sits behind the wheel. "It's done fool. Fuck that two in critical and we got the other two niggas, let's go." said Lump. "Let's get rid of this shit right now cause I'm tired and I ain't been to sleep all day." said Allante'. "We good now." said Melvo.

❊❊❊❊❊❊❊❊❊❊❊❊❊❊❊❊❊❊❊❊❊❊❊❊❊❊❊❊❊❊

12 A.M.
ALLANTE'S BEDROOM

Allante' lays on his bed, on his back sleeping. Heather walks into the room locking the door behind herself. Seeing Allante' sleep, Heather crawls on the bed over him, unbuckling his jeans. She reaches into his underwear pulling out his dick. She slowly places it inside of her mouth and his dick begins to grow inside of her mouth.

Allante' wakes up startled and pushes her head back pulling his dick out of her mouth. "What are you doing?"
"I'm sucking your dick."
"Nawl, Shorty." Allante shook his head.
"Nawl Shorty what, you eat my pussy."
"That's different." Tilting her head, "How? ... Look, I got a one-year old baby and I'm sixteen years old but I'm a grown azz woman and you my man and we're in your bedroom AND I want to suck your dick... NIGGA this is MY" dick nigga." staring at him intensely he could tell she was serious and meant every word she said. "We alone Allante' and I want to do you like you do me... no I'm not a freak but I'm giving it to you...all that I have is yours...my mind, body, and soul; and before you even ask NO I don't talk about the shit I do with you to nobody. I know you don't talk to you boys about how you fuck me, do you?"
"Hell no, that's me and you."
"Okay then, let me suck your dick." she smiled.

Allante leaned back smiling and said, "Okay then ...but you better suck it good and don't be bullshitting." Heather kisses the head of his dick with her soft lips opening her warm wet mouth taking some of him in. As his dick grow to full length much quicker than she thought she gags and takes him out of her mouth. "It's too big for me to get it all in, I ain't no pro."

Sly Allante' laughs and says" I could've to you that baby but don't worry about it cause you my pro." She places his dick back into her mouth bobbing her head up and down on his dick, fast then slow, twisting her mouth and wetting his dick. The more she sucks the more she gets turn on. Her pussy begins to throb, she wants him inside of her, and that makes her dick sucking skills that much better. Filled with excitement, Allante' grabs the blanket with his hands telling Heather that he is almost about to cum because he doesn't want to cum in her mouth he tried his best to move back quickly and as he does cum shots up on her face.

Embarrassed, he began, "I'm sorry...I----." She laughs, and he begins laughing with her. She grabs his washcloth going to the bathroom to wipe her face off, then she comes back out sitting beside him grabbing his dick washing it off. Looking him in the eyes. "Are you gon kiss me now?"
"Hell no!" He laughs.

Allante' leans in kissing her lips, their tongues find one another. Young dick, young dick, doesn't take long to recuperate and Allante's dick is rock hard again. She takes off her clothes and he laid down on his back on the bed, she straddles him. "Where is Josh?" She whispers back "In the room with your mother." She slowly lowers herself on his dick until he disappears inside of her. On the CD player Rihanna's song "Work" comes on and Heather leans back allowing herself to be flat on the bed for support.

As the song begins to say, work-work-work-work-, she begins gyrating her hips, winding and grinding her body up and down and around on his dick. She's popping her pussy on his dick like a female Jamaican dancer. "Work, work, work, work, work..." Is playing as she rocks back and forth. In her mind she's saying, "I'mma drain this niggas dick." In his mind he's saying, "Nigga you better not cum too fast!" Heather wins again, and he cums inside of her. She collapses on top of him, and they fall to sleep together holding on to one another.

✱✱✱✱✱✱✱✱✱✱✱✱✱✱✱✱✱✱✱✱✱✱✱✱✱✱✱✱✱

KEISHA'S HOUSE 11P.M.

"Breaking news, two men are now dead at Sinai/Grace Hospital on the west side of Detroit. Good evening, I'm Tina Dance. In the latest startling revelation two young men were found dead in their hospital beds from nails of a pneumatic nail gun to their face and heads. Police are looking for two black males who apparently dressed up as night janitors and walked right into the victim's room and murdered them. In a startling twist, the two men were involved in the shooting early yesterday morning at the Blue Lounge Room on Fenkell Street. Two others from that incident remain in critical condition from that incident. There were no officers at the door of these victim's room. City hall is going to have to come up with a lot of answers. This is Tina Dance, Eyewitness news…"

"Did you hear that shit Lump? Somebody wanted them niggas bad." said Keisha. "Yeah they was fucking with the wrong people. You got to know who you fucking with out here. Niggas ain't scared to bust them guns, and if you beefing with some niggas, how you gone be out partying? They must have thought that shit was sweet." said Lump. "But damn, it's been a lot of shit happening around where y'all live, be careful…"

Keisha grabs Lump's dick. "Don't hurt Mr. Goodbar." he said. Lump smacks her on her ass.
"We don't be slipping over there. If you ain't from around there, you gon stick out like a deer in a pack of lions. Keisha, when you gone give me some head?" Lump playfully controlled her head by her ponytail, "When you eat my pussy and don't worry, it tastes like strawberries."
"I don't like strawberries, I like peaches and cream."
"It can taste like that too if you want it too."
"We gon have to see what we can work out."

THE NEXT DAY
T'S HOUSE
DEQUINDRE STREET

"Here's the money for the first twenty joints. Said T. "Here's another twenty man that was fast. "Said Allante'. "When you got good work, it goes fast. I should have this gone in about two days."
"Bet, we got more. Hey T, let me ask you something, my dad said you got a lot of houses."
"Yeah, I do, why?"
"I'm trying to get into Real Estate, and get some of that commercial property downtown but right now, I'm trying to get a house for me and my boys on Outer Drive."
"I can help you with that nephew I got a Real Estate Broker who can fix the papers for you. When you trying to do it?"
"As soon as possible."
"I'll tell her to pull up some houses on Outer Drive, and I'll go look at them with you."
"Cool, I saw one on West 6 Mile and Outer Driver that I want to look at."
"I'll make sure she gets that one."
"Thanks, Unc!"
"You're doing way more at your age than I was when I was your age Allante'. If you need any advice about anything, call me.
"Aye, I got a fight down at Cobo Hall this Saturday. Come out if you can."
"I'll be there."

****

EUROPEAN CAR DEALERSHIP
WOODWARD AVE
BETWEEN 6 AND 7 MILE

Allante' walked around the showroom admiring all of the luxury cars. A voice called out "Can I help you sir?"

"I'm just looking."

"Your name's Allante' right?"

"How you know that?"

"I follow all Detroit boxing, you got a fight coming up."

"Yeah, Saturday down at Cobo Hall."

"You ready?"

"I'm always ready."

"Do you know who you fighting?"

"Yeah, some dude out of Lansing named Floyd …or something like that…it don't really matter cause I'mma crush him."

"What round?"

"First."

"Why, you be betting or something? Added Allante'.

"I do a little something."

Allante' sounded as if he stood ten feet tall, "Well I guarantee you 1st round! I'mma make a statement!"

"You see anything you like?" asked the owner.

"Yeah… I like this right here."

"It's nice but it costs."

"How much?"

"$80,000.00."

"So, you own this place?"

"Yeah."

"C'mon let's talk I want in and to tell you truthfully I could buy it flat out, but that would send me straight to jail." Allante looked the man dead in his eyes so he could see how serious he was. "So, can we work something out, where you get extra money and fix me up a car note?"

"Come on in my office young man cause I'm in the business of selling cars.... so, let's talk."

40 MINUTES LATER

"What you gon do with the Cutlass?" asked the dealership owner. "I brought this from my mother and it's my first car so I can't let it go but I'mma drive this and come back and get the Cutlass later. The car note gonna be paid every month on time." The salesman chuckled, "I'm sure it will. Enjoy it." Allante' hopped in, "Thank you."

IN FRONT OF HEATHER'S HOUSE

Allante' is blowing the horn. Heather looks out of her bedroom window. Allante' rolls down the tinted window on the passenger side leaning over his seat. Heather smiles upon noticing it's her man. She runs out of her room downstairs and out of the front door. The Matte Black Range Rover sits pretty looking real mean. "Go get Josh, let's go for a ride."

"Alright, give me ten minutes."

****

SITTING IN THE BUTTER COLORED LEATHER PASSENGER SEAT WITH JOSH IN HER LAP

Heather's leaning back and smelling the new leather scent of the Range Rover interior. "How did you get this?" Heather rubbed her hands along the console while testing out the touchscreen monitor.
"I worked out a deal with the car owner, he be coming to my fights. You like it?"
"I want it. I know I'll look good in this motherfucker! This shit feel like we riding on air."
"Beautiful, I got some stuff I need you to take care of."
"What you need?"
"This ain't for me, it's for you."
He added, "I'mma give you $3,500.00 dollars and I want you to open a checking and savings account for yourself.

Put $1,500.00 in the savings and $2,000.00 in the checking. I also want you to get a safety deposit box. I'mma start giving you money every week to put in your account for you and Josh. You can act like the money come from you doing hair every week. When you open this account they gon start sending you credit cards and you can use the cards and build up your credit. I got some money I want you to put in that box in case something happens to me, you'll be straight."

Heather frowned then said, "Don't be talking about in case something happens to you."

"I just want to put shit in order and I want to make sure you're growing. Listen to this, if with me being in your life, you don't grow, and become a better woman. I don't deserve to have you. I'm on some real shit right now. Don't ever accept in your life less than what I do for you, and how I treat you. If a man ain't adding to your life, he don't deserve you. You gonna do everything you set your heart and mind too. Let's go to Red Lobster. You hungry?"

"Yeah."

GREENFIELD ROAD

"Why you so quiet?" asked Allante'. "Just thinking." responded Heather. "About what?" "All this stuff that's happening around your way. I don't want nothing to happen to you."

Heather looks into Allante's eyes. Allante' said, "You ain't gotta worry about me Shorty cause I ain't doing nothing."

"You already changed my life Allante'."

"What you say?"

"I said you already changed my life. I'm already better. I'm graduating this year and finishing Cosmetology school. I got a car, my son good, my mother good, and I' m good. I just want you to be good…"

She added, "I started no to even go to the mall the day that I met you. I feel like I can do anything now." She could feel the real love between them. "You know I'm your number one fan! Well, me and Josh your number one fans. I'mma make sure you make it. Come on let's go. I got to take care of some shit, I'mma drop y'all off."

IN FRONT OF ALLANTE' MOTHER HOUSE

Allante' pulls up in front of his mother's house and Deborah is looking out the window seeing him getting out of the Range Rover. Seeing her son get out of the S.U.V. her heart drops and sadness is in her eyes; however, she holds back the tears that have filled her eyes. Allante' opens the door with his key opening it walking into the house closing the door behind him.

Deborah didn't allow him to enter the house good before she asked…
"Whose S.U.V. is that?"
"It's mines…I bought it."
"From where, where did you get the money?"
"I----… his mother cut him off quick.
"Do you really think I'm stupid, what the hell are you doing, you selling drugs!?"
"Nawl."
"Whoever let you buy that car is up to no good. You only sixteen years old. You thought you would

come in here driving that, and what, where did you get the money to buy it?"

"I can't tell----

"Then you gotta go."

Allante' dropped his head.

"I don't know what you're doing, but you can't do it here…"

"I didn't bring nothing in here and I don't do nothing here Ma." he tried to plead his case.

"I saw the clothes and I didn't say nothing. You said the money you gave me came from some work you did; she stared him down in disgust.

I work for the United States government. I'm not going to lose this house and all that I have worked for or your brothers because of things you are doing, no! Get your shit and get out! You are breaking my heart. I know you're doing something wrong." She starts crying her eyes out. Allante' walks up the stairs to his room and begins placing his clothes in a few gym bags. Allante' goes back and forth from his Range Rover to his house placing his things inside of the S.U.V., and on his last trip out of the house he looked into his brothers' room as they slept.

On his was out the front door, he turns to his mother and said, "I love you Ma, I just wanted to take care of you and Arraja and Andre." His mother violently shook her head no and told him, "I can't allow you to be under my roof, and know you're doing things that might get you killed. Money doesn't mean that much to me. Your brothers look up to you Allante' and they want to be just like you. She said tapping her chest. You have too much influence on them and they're not going to follow what you're doing as long as I live!"

She added, "I love you, but my love is not blind. Change what you're doing before it's too late just look at your father's life..." Allante' kisses his mother on her cheek before walking out of the front door hopping into his Range Rover.

ALLANTE' DRIVING AROUND THE CITY

Glock in his lap, Allante' has been riding around for two hours finding himself downtown at the Westin hotel in the Renaissance on Jefferson near Hart Plaza. "Yeah, let me get a suite."
"How many days sir?" asked the reservationist. "A week."
"Smoking or nonsmoking?"
"Nonsmoking."
"Okay sir, at $150.00 dollars a night, for seven days that total's $1,050.00."
"Here goes $1,100.00, keep the change."
"Thank you, sir."
She added, "Here's your key, room 203. Have a nice day, and thanks for staying at Westin."

INSIDE HIS SUITE

Allante' Is laying on the couch and or the first time in hours he is paying close attention to his cell phone that has been buzzing on vibrate for about the last three hours or more… missed calls from Heather, Lump, Melvo and his father fill his phone memory. Allante's mind returns to the conversation he shared with his mother. He can see the disappointment in her eyes. Confused about what he is feeling he closed his eyes drifting to sleep. Tomorrow, he knows will be brand new day.

THE NEXT MORNING

Fresh out of the shower dressed in a black Gucci Polo style shirt with green and red on the collar, black Gucci jeans and black Gucci loafers Allante' is walking to his Range Rover when his cell phone begins ringing. "Hello?" Heather snapped.
"Why are you not answering your phone and where are you at?" asked Heather.
"I'm downtown at the Westin."
"What are you doing down there?"
"My mother put me out."
"What? Why? Why you ain't call me? Why you ain't come over here?"
"I just got to get my head right… I'm good."
"But why you ain't come over here? You sleep over here all the time and my mother wouldn't have said nothing."

"I needed to be by myself Heather...." He then continued, "I'm on my way to school. I'm good Shorty... I'mma come pick you up at lunch time so be ready."

"Alright, I love you."

"I love you too."

NORTHWESTERN HIGH SCHOOL

Allante' pulls up next to the smoke colored 760, and platinum S550. The Range is mean. Lump and Melvo both smile upon seeing him pull up. "Fool that muthafucka mean! I called you all day yesterday, what's up?" asked Lump.

"Mannnnn Ma Dukes put me out last night."

"What?" asked Melvo. "She saw the Range and wasn't going for it."

"Why you ain't come over our house fool you know our house is yours." said Lump. "I went downtown and got a suite at the Westin. I'm good Mo... that shit just fucked me up. I'mma call her later on. Oh yeah T gave me the money for them one joints, I gave him twenty more. We'll split the money up later on." said Allante'. "Bet! I got to get to Homeroom, that bitch Mrs. Gray be on my line. I'll holler at y'all later." said Lump. They all walked into the school splitting up going to their own classes.

DETECTIVE CAMPBELL IN HER CAR

Driving in a gold Ford Taurus Detective Campbell is stopped at the traffic light at on West Grand Blvd. looking over into the High School parking lot she notices a smoke colored 760 BMW, a platinum S550 Mercedes Benz, and a matte black Range Rover. "Now I know teachers don't make enough to be driving luxury cars like those." Campbell said to herself. She makes a note to check and see who owns the cars.

Heading to the neighborhood of Livernois and Puritan to try and collect more information from citizens on this sudden burst of crime, she hears on the radio the promotion of the boxing match on Saturday at Cobo Hall and as a boxing fan she makes it a mental note to attend the fight.

CODY HIGH SCHOOL

It's 11:30 a.m. when Allante' pulls up in front of Heather's school. Heather, Keisha and Bree are walking out of the front door when they notice Allante' pull-up. "Bitch, that nigga on 1000." said Keisha. "Look at him, shidddd he know all eyes on him." said Bree. "Hey Alla!" said Bree and Keisha in unison. "What's up?" responded Allante'. Heather walks to the passenger side climbing into the Range. "I'll holler at y'all later, I'm ready Bae." She said goodbye to her girls.

"You alright Baby?" she asked Allante'.
"Yeah, that shit just fucked me up. That's my Mother. You know how I feel about her."
"She'll come around."
"Nawl Heather, she meant that shit."
"You know you ain't got to stay at no damn hotel. Come home with me…"

"Where you want to eat?" asked Allante' trying to change the subject, his cell phone begins to ring. "Hello? What's up Unc?"
"I'll have that money tomorrow, something came through." said T. Trying his best to sound excited.
"That's fast…yeah Unc I'll shoot through there no doubt … it's just a lot going on right now…plus my mother put me out last night. Although she could only hear one side of the conversation Heather could hear the hurt in Allante's voice as he spoke. Yeah, I brought a Range Rover and when she saw it she told me that I had to go."
"You alright?"
"I'm good."
"Look, I own a house on W. Outer Drive. Come over and see me."
"When?"
"Now, if you're not busy."
"I'll be right over." Allante' ended the call and he turns to Heather. "That's my father's partner, I need to stop over his house. You cool?"
"I'm on your hip so what we gon do?"

She added, "I'm staying with you, wherever you going, I'm going. Wherever you sleep, I'm sleeping with you." Allante' smiled and said, "Well that's good cause I'mma get a house sooner than later and that's actually what I got to holler at him about."

SCENE 4:
THE PLANS OF THE PRIDE

T'S HOUSE

"What's up Unc, this is my girl Heather." introduced Allante'. "Hello." greets Heather.
"Hey, I'm T. you all have a seat." He points them to the living room sofa. T continues, "So listen, Alla I got a 4-bedroom, 3-bathroom home, on West Outer Drive between 6 and 7 Mile. "I own it straight out and this is what I'm willing to do for you cause we family. I don't have to go through a bank to sale it. I can make what's called a land contract. That's when the sale of the house is between you and me. Now what I would do is turn the deed over to you and you pay me for the house. It's a $250,000.00-dollar home." Allante' looked at T. "I want it.

We'll have the contract drawn out by my lawyer and we'll work out the payments. Do you already have a lawyer?" Allante' responded shrugging his shoulders, "Nawl."
"Get one; even when you don't have anything going on, you want to be on point. I'll give you some names and you can meet with them and retain the one you want. Listen here you always want a layer on call. Here, here's the keys to the house."

"Unc, man it's like you from heaven."
"Your father is my brother, you my family. Hey, I got a proposition I want to talk to you and your friends about. Bring them over tomorrow when you come about the money."
"Alright, we getting ready to go check this house out." Patting his nephew on the back as he stood up, "It's your now." Allante' smiles as and Heather leave the house on their way to check out their new home.

SINALOA, MEXICO

"Who the fuck killed my brother?" Said Puncho Diaz. "We don't know yet Puncho and the police don't have any suspects. We stick out in the area too much, so we are working on a way to find out who's who over there." said Joker.

"I lost too much fucking money and product! FUCK! I want somebody fucking dead. You tell our guys over there if they don't bring me news of a dead nigga or niggas over there who did this, I will kill their families over here!"
"I'm on it Puncho."

DEBORAH CAMPBELL & C.I. (CONFIDENTIAL INFORMANT)

"So, I want to know who is who in his area." asked Campbell. "It's a couple of dudes over there getting a little money. It's a dude name Ru-boi who got the loud on lock, and a dude name Deuce who push the dope over here. They the ones who got crews over this way. As far as coke, it's wide open. People smoke crack so they gonna get it from whoever got it. It's a lot of young-ins who sling." said the C.I. "Well, keep your ears open and if you hear anything get in touch with me, I'll let Jones over in Narcotics know that you're cooperating." Campbell ended the conversation.

WEST OUTER DRIVE

"There it go right there Bae. Oh my God, it's gorgeous! Look how green the grass is in the front of the yard!" Slowly Allante' pulls into the driveway. "There's a two-car garage in the back, I can see it from here." The two-story brick house looks immaculate from the outside. Allante' and Heather get out of the Range and walking to the front door, he puts the key in the door opening it.

Together they walk into the front foyer of the house and Heathers' eyes become big as she looks around. "This house is the shit!" The couple walk through the living room into the kitchen there is a half bathroom on the first floor off of the hallway. Heading back to the front of the house they walk upstairs. At the top of the stairs to the right sit's a full bathroom. Directly down the hallway sit's one bedroom. To the left, halfway down the hall, sit's another bedroom. On the right past the bathroom sit's the Master bedroom. As they walk into the

Master bedroom, Heather smiles. "Damn Bae this room is so big! Look Bae, it's a bathroom right here in the bedroom." Heather looks out of the bedroom patio window at the backyard. "Oh my God the backyard is so big Allante' and it has a tall privacy fence."

"So, you like it?" Allante smiled at Heather. "Hell yeah and it has carpet all the way through… this house is nice Allante'. I could put all kind of furniture in here." Heather walked around the empty space rubbing her hands along the walls. "So, you know how to decorate?" Sensing her confidence Allante' laughed as he spoke.

"Boy stop playing, I'll hook this house up." "Alright, we'll see. Let's look at the basement." They walk down the stairs to the basement door off the kitchen and walk down into a full basement completely finished. One bedroom sit's in the back of the right side and another full bathroom sits off to the left with a small room that has a washer and dryer in it. A basement door leading to the backyard is close to the front of the basement.

"This is the kind of shit my mother supposed to be living in." said Allante'. "You're going to be a World Champion Alla, you'll get her one." As they walk back upstairs, Alla looks at Heather, and begins, "I need you to be on your shit."

"What you mean?" She looked at him confused. "Here go the money for the checking and Savings Account. This right here is $30,000.00 dollars. This is all I got on me right now. I need a nice bedroom set. Don't get no cheap shit, but listen, you can't spend more than $9,000.00 dollars in one spot. Just do what I tell you. Get a bedroom set with a flat screen for our bedroom and get a living room set. Write the address down and have them deliver it today. Make sure you know the time so you can be here. Here go a key, when I come back, I'll give you come more money so you can get the rest of the stuff we need.

Come on, I'mma take you to get something to eat, and I'mma drop you back off at school."
"I got you Babe, I'mma make you proud." Heather said beaming with pride. Allante' walked behind Heather with his hands around her waist as they walked out of the house. "Don't bring no weak shit in here, if you do I'mma laugh yo ass out!" Allante' could barely talk he was laughing so hard,

WESTIN HOTEL

Back inside of the hotel room, Allante' takes $100,000.00 dollars from the money he got back from T for the twenty kilos. The remaining $300,000.00, Allante' keeps inside the gym bag ready to give it to Lump and Melvo. One would get $100,000.00, and the other brother would get

$200,000.00, and they will rotate that number until all three get $400,000.00 dollars apiece for the eighty kilos. Sitting on the bed, Allante' is thinking better yet wishing that the situation with him and his mother were different. Thinking about his little brothers he feels as if he's let them down. He knows that he's really the only male in their lives, and now he's no longer present in the house with them.

Standing up he grabs his Glock, placing it inside his Velcro gun holster that he has on his waist. With the bag of money in his other hand he secures the room and then heads out on his way to Lump and Melvo's house.

SWANSON FUNERAL HOME

At the last funeral of the young men who were killed at the Sinai Hospital, Detective Campbell sits by a broken-hearted mother who lost her only child. "Mrs. Powell, I'm so sorry. From what we've learned this was not drug related. I believe all of this stems from an incident at Dot Etta's where Nate Willis was shot. This is all related to that and I'm working hard to find the killers of your son." said Detective Campbell.

"I don't understand these kids. They take lives so easily. My son has a daughter who won't know her father now. It's got to stop... it's too much... please find them." responded Mrs. Powell. "I'm doing everything I can Mrs. Powell."

FIRST BANK OF DETROIT

"Mrs. Brown that does it. Now you have an active checking and savings account with us. In about a week or two you should receive a box of personal checks at your home. They'll be just like the ones you picked out. Also, your ATM card should come in about two weeks. Be mindful now that a lot of credit card companies are going to be trying to get you to sign up with them. While credit cards are nice to have spending money you may not have can get out of control so use caution. Also, here's the key to your safety deposit box they're located in that room over there to the left. The room is made available during our normal working hours. You'll always have to sign in before going into the room. Are there any questions?" asked the female bank manager. "No ma'am" answered Heather.
"Thank you for your business, if you need anything come back and see us." Heather smiled wide.
"Thank you so much ... I just feel like I've really accomplished something that's very important."
"You did young lady, there are very few people your age that are thinking about a banking account."

LUMP AND MELVO'S MOTHER HOUSE

"Mo, here is y'all part of the money from the work. It's $300,000.00 in here. One of y'all get $100,000.00 and the other gets $200,000.00 dollars. T said he'll have the money for the second twenty bricks tomorrow, well do the same thing and

whoever gets the $100,000.00 dollars today will get the $200,000.00 tomorrow." said Allante' "What about yours?" asked Lump. "I'll get it on the one after that. Hey, he said he got a proposition he want to talk to us about tomorrow. I told him all three of us would come through. "Bet." Melvo added.
"Oh yeah, T sold me a house."
"Where is it at?" Lump asked. "It's on Outer Drive. That motherfucker laying like that man. I took Heather over there and we checked it out."
"What's up with the one we supposed to be getting?" asked Lump. "I gotta go look at that one on Sunday at 1:30 p.m."
"I'm going wit you, I ain't doing shit." said Lump.
"Bet." Melvo turned and asked, "Y'all trying to go to the movies tonight? I was going with Bree." "We can do that." said Lump. "I'm good with that." said Allante'.
"Let's go to the one on Schaefer and 6 Mile." said Melvo.

Allante's cell phone begins ringing. "What's up beautiful?" Sounding out of breath; "I just came back from bank and I got it all done; I'm so excited…thank you." said Heather. "You sound happy azz shit." said Allante'. "I am. I'm going to pick up Josh, and then I'm going to get the bedroom set and flat screen. I'll be at the house after that waiting on them to deliver the stuff." Heather said with excitement. "We all going to the movies tonight. I'mma come pick you and Josh up after I make a few runs."

"Okay, I love you babe."

"I love you too Shorty."

MOVIE THEATER

The movie that the crew went to see was called "Life" featuring Eddie Murphy and Martin Lawrence. Allante', Lump and Melvo along with Heather, Josh, Keisha and Bree all walked out of the movie theater laughing. "Mane, that nigga Bernie Mac funny as shit, that was fucked up how they got jammed up over some shit they didn't do." said Lump. "Niggas getting jammed up for shit they ain't do all the time fool. This shit ain't fair out here." said Melvo.

"Aye there go Ru-boi and Deuce... What's up y'all?". "What up doe Alla, what's up y'all? I see y'all out and about." spoke Deuce. "What up doe?" said Ru-boi. He then adds, "Y'all looking good out here aye that joint was funny as hell."

"Yeah that shit was good... so what's up wit y'all?" asked Lump. "Shit, we just enjoying the last couple weeks of getting ready for the summer. It's a lot of shit been happening around the way. Po Po been riding around, it's hot out here. Niggas is out here talking." said Deuce. "What they saying?" asked Allante'. "That's what we need to holler at y'all about." said Ru-boi. "Aiight we'll meet up." said Melvo. "Hey, dude with y'all?" asked Lump "Nawl." answered Deuce and Ru-boi. Allante' turns to Lump, "What's up?"

"I'm about to find out. A fool! What the fuck you keep looking at us for?!" The two dudes standing together on the sidewalk glared at them, "What the fuck you talking bout, nigga I'm looking at you!" Wasting absolutely no time at all…

"Smack!" Lump hurls off smacking the first dude with his gun. Melvo swings his gun at the second guy, smacking him with it upside his jaw.

"Y'all go to the car!" yelled Allante' to the girls. The dude that Melvo hit had fell to the ground before he could get up to his feet, Allante' kicked him in his face. Ru-boi and Deuce began stumping and punching the other guy with Lump. Seeing that they are outnumbered the two men being attacked quickly got to their feet and fled the scene without looking back.

As if she is frozen in time Heather is still standing there with Josh, when Allante' turns his head and he immediately becomes upset. "Hey, what the fuck I tell you to do?" asked Allante'. Gulping down a large lump in her throat Heather responds, "To go to the car." Allante' balls his fist in frustration. "So why you still standing there… go to the car like I said!" Heather grabs Josh's hand

leading him to the Range Rover. Allante' turned to Ru0boi and Deuce, "Y'all know them niggas?"
"They stay by Wyoming round where them niggas got killed stay at." responded Deuce. "Fool, I ain't going for that!" said Lump. "Let's go, too many people looking at us." Said Melvo. "We out, call me later, Alla!" said Lump. "Aiight, I'll see y'all later. Good looking."
"Y'all know we family, we'll holla at y'all."

IN THE RANGE

"Look at me, when you see drama and I tell you to do something just do it. If I got a problem with a nigga, I need to have my eyes on them. If you there, I got to make sure you safe first. That makes me take my eyes off my man. When I tell you to move you MOVE! Whatever, I tell you to do, do it. Do it the way I tell you, don't do it the way you wanna do it. Do you hear me?" Nodding her head, "Yes." Answered Heather. "My responsibility is to protect you, we good?"
"Yeah."

BACK AT THE HOTEL
ROOM 203

Allante' is in the shower, Heather gets in behind him. Reaching around him she grabs his dick massaging it in her hand making his young Lion dick grow and he's about to crush his Lioness. Turning around facing her water is bouncing off of their bodies. They stare into one another's eyes before their lips come together. Allante's hand lightly grabs Heather's breast and her nipples instantly become hard. He lifts her left leg up, and she places both of her arms around his neck lifting herself up, wrapping her legs around his waist. He grabs his dick, sliding it inside of her. Her back is up against the back of the shower wall. He is now moving in and out of her as her body is bouncing up and down.

Her bouncing becomes more vigorous, her facial expressions change from pain to pure pleasure, she begins bouncing up and down faster and faster. Allante' leans forward, thrusting his dick inside of her releasing his sperm into her hot wet pussy. They both are breathing heavily. He releases her from his embrace, walking out of the shower dripping wet. Heather follows behind him like the girl in love that she is.

In the bedroom Josh is laying on the bed sleep. Heather is on her knees on the bed behind Allante' rubbing lotion onto his back and shoulders. "Why we ain't go to the house tonight?"
"I want to get the house cleaned first before we start living in it." She notices that he said we and she begins to smile. "I ain't mean to talk to you like that, but anything could happen out there, and you and Josh was right there in the line of fire and if I can't protect you then I don't deserve you. You got

to do what I tell you and don't have no complex about that. I'm not moving off of ego, if something happen to y'all because of some shit I'm doing I'mma be fucked up Heather."
"I understand Allante".

1824 ROSELAWN

"Man look at my muthafuckin' face! The whole right side of my face is fucked up. I want to kill all them motherfuckers!" said Sam Brisborn.
"I think my ribs are broken." said Kevin Draper. "What happened?" asked Sonny Brisborn who is Sam's brother. "We was outside of the movie theater and this nigga asked me why I was looking at him. I told the nigga I was looking at him and basically fuck him! He swung on me and the niggas he was with jumped us. I want to know who the fuck they are." said Sam. "The tall dude's name is Deuce. He be hustling down by Livernois and Puritan. The other niggas probably from around that way too." said Kevin. "We could ride through and shoot the whole motherfucking area up." added Odell. "I'm trying to see them niggas." said Sam. "We got to be right cause them niggas ain't faking down there. They saying them the niggas that killed Nate and all them. If you ain't trying to go all the way Mo, don't even open that up." said Kevin. "I can't let them niggas get away with that." Sam said looking at himself in the mirror.

THE NEXT DAY
T'S HOUSE

Allante', Lump and Melvo are setting on the living room couch while T is sitting on top of his coffee table. "It's some fake Arabs in Dearborn, over by Warren and McGraw they got a stash house over there with a lot of heroin and money in it. I'm talking a easy six to seven million cash and fifteen to twenty bricks of yayo." said T.

Hearing the figures, all off the boys whistled with excitement. "We need that!" said Lump. "It's sweet but you got to be careful because it's in their community. They stick together." said T. "So how many people in the joint?" asked Allante'. "If y'all down, I got all the details." said T. They all look at one another. "We good to go." said Allante'. "Well listen…."

ALLANTE IN THE RANGE ROVER
USING THE PHONE

"Hey Mo, we need to holla at you and Ru-boi. We got something we want to put before y'all…"
"Aiight, meet us at the Coney Island, on Livernois at eight o'clock tonight…Aiight." ended Allante'.

CONEY ISLAND

"Mo, we got another lick my people put us up on but it's going to take more than us to pull it off." said Allante'. Deuce and Ru-boi are sitting across the table from Lump, Allante', and Melvo. "We listening." said Deuce. "We got to move where we can get 6 to 7 million cash and fifteen to twenty Ki's of raw. Deuce you know the street value that is at least nine million. The money would be one point four million apiece for us. We don't want none of the raw, but Deuce, if you want some of that shit we will holla at my people to see how to work it out." finished Allante'. "Shit, if the money is right I don't need nothing else so when we gon do this shit?" asked Deuce. "We gone have to move fast, cause we gotta do it by next Wednesday." said Melvo. "We in homeboys... now how we gon do it?" asked Ru-boi. "Listen..."

SATURDAY 2 P.M
COBO HALL

"You ready son?' asked Coach Logan. "I was born for stuff like this coach." answered Allante'. "It's like eight to ten thousand people out there." said Logan. Allante' smiles, "He's gon be super embarrassed cause I'm crushing everybody that gets in front of me. I'm making a statement today!"
"Alright, let's go, you up! Said Logan. The commentator began, "Ladies and Gentlemen, here we are at the main event of the day! In the red corner he comes from Lansing, Michigan, weighing in at 135 pounds with an amateur record of eighty-two wins and three losses, Floyd Mays, Mays!"

The commentator then turned to face Allante'. "And in the blue corner, he comes out of Detroit's own Kronks Boxing Gym, weighing in at 135 pounds with an amateur record of ninety-three wins and zero defeats, your very own, Allante' Light, Light!"

The referee began, "Alright, I gave you my instructions in the locker room, obey my commands at all times, protect yourself at all times. Touch gloves if you want too… OKAY, LET'S GET IT ON!" Both fighters walked over to their corners and the bell rings. The commentator begins, "Here we go, Light moves to the right and forces Mays to move to his left which is awkward for him. Mays jabs and Light effortlessly moves his head.

Mays jabs again but yet again Light slips his jab! They are playing chess right now; and Light has yet to throw a punch! Mays jabs again. Light slips and pop! Oh, Light shoots a straight right and drops Mays! Mays is down! He takes a knee! The ref gives him a mandatory eight count!

Okay here we go! Light steps in, left jab! Left uppercut! Left hook, oh my God all with his left hand! He squats down, and hit's Mays with a hard right hand to the body! Mays bends over and Light hits him with a flurry of punches. Light leans to the right, and delivers a right hand to the body and a right uppercut to the chin which lift Mays head up!

Light caps it off with a beautiful left hook! It's over! He's out!" You can barely hear him over the roar of the crowd "The ref has just stepped in to stop it! It was a beautiful display of skills by this young phenom! You just saw the future of boxing folks, I hope you appreciated this artistry!"

Getting out of the ring, Allante' hears his name. He looks and sees his two little brothers and his mother. He also notices T, Heather and her girls sitting in the stands with Lump and Melvo. They're all standing up clapping and Allante' is smiling from ear to ear. Looking at his mother and little brothers Allante shouts to them, "I'll be right back... Let me go change!"

BACK IN THE STADIUM

Allante' kisses his mother on her cheek, he then hugs both his brothers. "You looked real good in there." said his mother. "Thank you, Ma."
"You tore him up!" said his little brothers.
"Y'all like that?" Allante' loved the praise from his biggest fans. "Yeah!" answered the brothers in unison. "Where y'all getting ready to go now?" asked Allante' looking at his mother. "We're going back home." answered his mother. "Can I take them to get something to eat?"
"We want to go Ma!" said the brothers.
"Alright bring them back by nine p.m."
"Okay, let's go."

HART PLAZA

The whole crew is walking to their cars in the underground parking garage. Lump began, "Where we going to eat?" Allante's little brothers look up at him, "We want some pizza Allante'."
"Let's go over to Greek Town; they got a joint over there called Pizza Papalis. They got seafood pizza, ham and pineapple pizza deep dish… whatever you like they got it." said Allante'.
Bree whined, "I'm hungry as hell."
Lump smiled, "It's on me cause my nigga crushed dat dude today; fool you looked good as shit in there today." Melvo joined in with his brother. "Yeah, you beat the fuck out of that nigga!" the whole crew agreed laughing heading over to Greek Town.

UNDERGROUND PARKING GARAGE

As detective Bernice Campbell walks to her car, she observes a smoke gray 760, black Range Rover, and a platinum S550, along with a group of young teens getting into the vehicles. "I know those are the same cars I saw in the parking lot at Northwestern High School. I'll go over there and run those tags this week. Ain't no way in hell, those are their cars." She is thinking to herself.

SUNDAY 1:30P.M
1713 OUTER DRIVE

"Fool we getting this joint. This shit just right for us. Big rooms and a lot of space!" said Melvo.

"I like this joint too!" said Lump. "So, this what y'all want? We ain't gotta go look at nothing else?" asked Allante'. "Nawl Slim, we good." said Melvo. Lump nods his head in agreement. "We'll holla at T's Real Estate agent, and get everything worked out. We got to put this shit together for this lick. We gon do it Tuesday." said Allante'. "We ready fool!" said Melvo. "I gotta make sure Deuce and Ru-boi on point cause this shit gotta go right."

TUESDAY 9:30 A.M
DEARBORN, MICHIGAN

"Mo, when they answer the door tell them you're here to check the led level in the paint. When you get in, let'em know you got to check every room. Mo, I'm calling your phone now…" The phone rings several times before Deuce answers, "Yo?" Allante' then said, "Now put the ear piece in so when you're in there we can hear you and you can tell us where everybody at while you're walking through the house.

Once you go through the house grab the nigga who with you and put your gun to his head and holla D.E.A.! We'll already be on our way in there. When you go in the door put this putty in the door lock. Mo, we coming in there guaranteed." said Allante'. "I'm ready." responded Deuce. Utility belt over his shoulder, Glock ready to rock, Deuce gets out of the van and walks to the front door of the house.

Knocking on the door a woman answers. "Hello ma'am, I'm here to check the led levels in the paint of your home." She lets him come inside. In the living room Deuce tells the twenty something year old girl that he has to check the entire house and the girl agrees. Speaking into his ear piece Deuce begins to describe what is going on inside of the house. "Nobody is inside the living room."

"Let's move y'all… Ru-boi, "Stay in the van and be ready to push this motherfucker when we come out." said Allante'. "I got y'all." said Ru-boi. Allante', Melvo, and Lump hop out the side of the van, and run to the first door. "Two men first bedroom on the left upstairs… all other rooms upstairs are clear." said Deuce in his earpiece.

Gun in hand the three young lions push the front door open. "D.E.A.!" shouts Deuce. Melvo sprints up the stairs where the two men lay startled from the sudden noise. Gun trained at the first guy's head, Melvo shouts, "Don't move or I'mma kill both of y'all!" Allante' and Lump run through the dining room and kitchen, opening the basement door. Lump has the pump and Allante' has his Glock .40. They make sure that the basement is clear before they run back upstairs to the second floor where they tie up the two men and girl.

The four Lions split up searching for the money and drugs. In the master bedroom Lump hollers out, "BINGO!" They all meet up in the room with smiles on their faces while staring at the shrink-wrapped money in bundles and the bricks of raw stacked in rows of four.

"Mo, go get the bags out of the van!" said Allante'. Melvo runs out to the van, coming back to hand the other three two gym bags each. They all fill up the gym bags with money and drugs before carrying it all down to the front door. "Mo put em to sleep." said Allante'. "Gotcha!" answered Lump.

"Come on y'all, let's put this shit in the van!" said Allante'. Lump pulls out a nail gun walking up the steps with the silent killer in his hand. As the girl and the two men look up with fear in their eyes, Lump squeezes the trigger over and over until death fills the room. Turning around, he runs down the stairs, and walks out of the door to the van climbing in the crew drives off.

"Dawg, that shit was sweet as a motherfucker!" shouted Deuce. "Now we got to get rid of this van." said Allante'. The young crew rode back across the line from Dearborn into the city of Detroit and the sighs of relief filed the air. They arrive at the Edison Utility Plant on Warren and Livernois. It's there that they ditch the van before climbing into the stolen cars that they have waiting for them heading back to the hood.

MOTEL
ON LINWOOD & W. GRAND BLVD
ROOM 206

"Now I know how the fuck y'all niggas be getting it!" Ru-boi eyed the caper like a savage hound. Shaking his head in disbelief, "Man how the fuck we get all of this money!" Deuce responded, "This the type of shit I'm talking about." Deuce then quoted the rap song singing at the top of his lungs, "I'm all the way up and nothing can stop me!"

"We got to count this money...aye break one of them joints open, it looks like they got'em in $100,000.00-dollar slabs. If that's the case it'll be easy for us to count this shit." said Allante'. "Yeah fool, this is a hundred g's" added Melvo. "Count that shit up and split it up. "Lump, this is twenty-five bricks of raw and I don't know how much this shit worth on the streets but we gon give it all to T!" said Allante'. "Cool mane." said Lump.

Deuce then said, "If this shit any good it's ten million easy in these streets. You can step on that shit at least five or six times and it'll still be a monster." Allante' asked, "Well what's up with y'all?" Melvo answered, "We gon give it to our old head like we said. "Unc put us down with the lick so that's his as far as I'm concerned" Allante' said looking around at the four-man crew. "Hell yeah!" said Lump. Ru-boi then said, "I don't even

know'em but hell yeah... I love him already!"
Deuce included, "I was just letting y'all know what
this shit worth. I'm cool with whatever we do."
"I'mma take this shit over there to him. Mo, I'll pick
my money up from you when I get back from
dropping this shit off." said Allante'. I got you
cuz!" said Lump.

T's HOUSE

"It was three people in the house, two dudes
and one broad. We had to wet'em. That joint was
easy though. It all went like you said. We used nail
guns to take em out so it wasn't no noise. We
haven't finished counting the money yet but this is
all yours it was twenty-five bricks in there." ended
Allante'.

T responded, "That's even more than I
thought but I'm glad everything went right. They
played me on some shit a month ago so I wanted to
fuck them over. "This shit ain't gone come back on
you is it?" asked Allante'. "I don't give a fuck about
them motherfuckers. They know what time it is. We
let them motherfuckers eat around here and they
was eatin' too goddamn much!" said T.

"Aye Unc, I was thinking about trying to buy
some of those buildings downtown in the Cass
Corridor. They got a lot of abandoned buildings
down there and if they're building downtown back

up then that property down there is going to be worth some money."

"You're right."

"Can you help me look into that?"

"Yeah, I'll holler at my Real Estate bitch; maybe we can be partners on something."

"That'll be cool… we went and saw the house on Outer Drive that the agent booked us to see. We told her we wanted it, Melvo and Lump really liked that joint." Nodding in agreement T half-smiled then said, "Yeah, she told me. She's working on the paperwork now. Y'all will be good in a few weeks to a month." Allante' knew they would be happy to get that news. "Heather is staying with me in the other house." T raised his eyebrows at that update.

"You're a lot more mature than I was at you age and you also got a lot more money than I had." T said with a light chuckle.

Placing a hand on his shoulder T looked down at Allante' and said, "Money make a lot of people think they invincible nephew, but the truth is, it makes them a target… always be alert."

"Got you Unc... I got to go pick up my money."

"Call me throughout the week to let me know you safe."

ALLANTE'S HOUSE

After having already picked up his portion of the money from Melvo, and Lump, Allante' arrived at their home. When he pulled up in the driveway, Heather's car is already there. Grabbing the gym bag full of money, he entered his home through the side door which leads to the kitchen. Walking through the kitchen, into the living room, he notices the living room set that Heather had brought and already set up in the house. It consisted of a lavender in color soft leather wraparound sofa suit with reclining captain's chairs, a mahogany wood coffee table with the glass top and cream and lavender layered curtains… or as she corrected him "drapes". Allante laughed about that moment in his head.

The home is still yet to be fully furnished however, little by little it is coming together and he was pleased; well that was until…Walking up the steps, Allante' glances in Josh's room smiling as he sees Josh's race car styled bed. Heather has Josh's room, decked out in a football theme, but he has the race car bed. 'Yeah she's a Bama.' thought Allante' to himself and shaking his head before laughing to himself and out loud.

Walking into the master bedroom, Heather is sitting on the middle of their big bed talking on her cell phone. On the carpet Josh is sitting playing with Allante's boxing gloves. Looking up noticing Allante' standing there, Josh begins smiling before getting up instantly to run to Allante'. Sitting his gym bags down on the floor, Allante' bends down to pick up little man. Heather is still talking on her phone analyzing Allante' and her son interact, showing his love for her son amazes her always.

"Girl I'll call you later, Alla here! ... Bitch that's right, I'mma suck his dick dry..." she laughed hysterically before ending her phone call. "Hey Babe!" said Heather excited. Allante' sits on the bed still holding Josh. "I'm tired azz shit... what you cook?" asked Allante'. "Some crab-cakes and stir-fry, do you want me to fix you a plate?" already knowing the answer.

"Yeah. When you come back, I need you to help me count this money." Allante rubbed his temples, "Okay..." answered Heather. She stands up making her way downstairs to fix his plate for him. Soon after, Heather is back upstairs with the plate of food in her hand, she stops in her tracks upon noticing the large piles of money spread all over their bed and sees Josh playing happily with the wrapped packages of money in his hands.

"How much is this supposed to be?" asked Heather in awe. "A lot. I don't want to tell you the number until after we count it...It should be $100,000.00 dollars in each pack that's $10,000.00 in each band. Go ahead and start counting it soon as I finish eating, I'll help you." Handing him his plate, Heather responds, "Yeah this is a lot of money.

Sitting down at the edge of the bed with his plate he asked, "So what did y'all two do to act busy today?" "Just picked up some more stuff for the house. This is a lot of work filling this house." she sighed. "Work? I thought you was laying like that; ain't you the interior decorator?" asked Allante' eating some of his food. "I am but this shit ain't easy picking out the right color."

Chewing and laughing Allante' almost choked, "Yeah cause I see that Bama ass bed you picked out for my lil man!" clearing his throat, "You got him football curtains and shit with a race-car bed…" Why you ain't get him a helmet bed?" asked Allante'. Looking puzzled and shrugging her shoulders Heather responded, "I ain't know they made them." Still trying to clear his throat Allante' was able to get out, "Yeah that's cuz you a Bama." Shaking his head, he added, "You know about hair and clothes, but you don't know shit about nothing else." Heather leaned in punching him in his arm playfully. "Yes, I do!" "Nawl, I'm just fucking with you. You gon be whatever you want to be in this world Heather, I got you."
"I love you so much." said Heather sincerely.

1 HOUR LATER

"This is $1,400,000.00 dollars! Oh my-fucking-GOD! All this fucking money… Damn ALLA!" said Heather. "Tomorrow morning, I got to go put this up. It's some stuff I'm going to show you. This right here is $150,000.00 dollars, I'mma put this in a paper bag and you put it in the Safety Deposit box tomorrow." said Allante' handing her the paper bag. "Alright." Heather nodded as he spoke. Allante' placed a sleeping Josh into his bed. Then he walks back inside of his room where he fucked Heather all over their king size bed until the early morning hours arrived.

SCENE 5:
EVEN THE HUNTERS ARE HUNTED... IN THE CIRCLE OF LIFE

2 WEEKS LATER
AMACO GAS STATION

Sitting inside his Cadillac CTS at the corner of Livernois and Puritan, Deuce is talking to his girl Alesha who's sitting in the passenger seat. A money green Chevrolet Impala pulls into the parking lot of the gas station. Two young black males jump out of the Impala with an AK47 and a Street-Sweeper approaching the Cadillac quickly. The shooters lift their rifles and begin shooting...The automatic weapons began singing a thunderous tune, bullets spraying and riddling the CTS unmercifully.

In a panic, Deuce puts his car in gear, speeding off feeling the bullet penetrate his right shoulder. Adrenaline pumping, he looks in the passenger seat to notice half of his girl's head missing. With his vision slowly fading the CTS swerves hitting a parked car. With his body leaning forward against the steering wheel, the horn blaring loudly, attention is drawn from each and every direction. People immediately begin pulling out their cell phones dialing 9-1-1. As time ticks, death is always seeking an opportunity to roar.

WEST 8 MILE
COMMERCIAL STORAGE UNIT

"This is where I keep my money. Inside these safes after I put this money inside it'll be about $3,000,000.00 in here. You're the only person in the world who know this. I got a lawyer because T taught me I should have one. The lawyer has a letter I wrote to my mother in case something happens to me. In the letter, I told her where the money is and that you know about it." said Allante' to Heather. "Why are you talking like this?" she frowned.
"Look, I'm a hustler Heather. Shit could go wrong at any time. Now can you handle this?"
"I think I can." She responded quietly. "Make sure my mother, brothers, you and Josh are safe."

Allante's cell phone begins to ring. "Aye, what's up homez? .... Where y'all at.... I'm on my way!" Allante' turn to look at Heather. "Look I gotta go, some shit came up." Quickly pulling her out off unit by the arm. "Is everything alright?"
"Nawl, my man Deuce got hit. Look, take the Range, I'mma get a cab. I'll see you later... keep your phone on." Allante' tossed her the keys as he ran up the hall. Hoping that he heard her Heather said, "Okay baby, be careful."

SINIA HOSPITAL
THE EMERGENCY ROOM

Total chaos is the only way to describe the scene unravelling in the overcrowded E.R. ward.

"CLEAR THE WAY!!!!!!!!!" YELLED THE ER TECH. WE HAVE A BLACK FEMALE JANE DOE DOA, SINGLE GUNSHOT WOUND TO HEAD…ONE BLACK MALE WITH WHAT APPEARS TO BE MULTIPLE ENTRY AND EXIT GUNSHOT WOUNDS… A SINGLE BULLET ENTRY WOUND BACK RIGHT SHOULDER ALL THE WAY THROUGH!!!!! ENTRY WOUND LOWER RIGHT ABDOMEN. JOHN DOLE MALE IS UNRESPONSIVE NO VITALS!!! PROCEED TO USE THE DIFIBULATOR CLEAR!!! NO PULSE! CLEAR! AGAIN! CLEAR! WE HAVE A PULSE! PUT HIM ON THE OPERATING TABLE!! CUT HIS CLOTHES OFF!!!!!"

EMERGENCY ROOM HALLWAY

Lump, Melvo and Ru-boi are standing against the wall. Deuce's mother Sharon, his little brother and his two little sisters are sitting in chairs crying, waiting for news from the doctors on Deuce's condition. Allante' walks into the emergency room seeing his best friends accompanying Deuce's mother and sisters. "Mo, what the fuck happened?" asked Allante'.

"Somebody hit him at the gas station. His girl is dead. They shot half her head off man." said Ru-boi. "Well what the fuck do we know right now?" asked Allante'. "The young dude that work at the gas station said it was a green Impala. He said two dudes jumped out and lit the car up. It was at least three of them. It might be those niggas from the movie, I don't know." said Lump. Ru-boi added, "He wasn't beefing with nobody else because he would of told me homey."

"Damn, Heather gone be fucked up. His girls name is Alesha. Heather be doing her hair. What's up with Deuce?" asked Allante'. "We don't know yet, they been in there for a little bit over a hour." said Melvo. Allante' looks over at Deuce's mother and sisters, walking over to them. "Hello Mrs. Washington. I'm sorry about your son, but he's gone pull through. We are going to find out what happened and who did it and whatever Deuce needs we gone get it.

Is it anything you need?" asked Allante'. "No baby, just pray that my baby makes it. I need my son to make it." answered Sharon as Deuce's little brother Greg walked up. Right behind Greg are the two Homicide Detectives working the area for similar shootings Bernice Campbell and Justin Brooks. Campbell passed by the young men standing on the wall and they all eye her. She is dressed in her uniform black slacks and white top. Melvo eyes her up and down. His eyes lock in on her fat round ass. "Excuse me, you need to take your eyes off my ass." Melvo respond, "Nawl, I was just thinking about something." adjusting his hand in his pants. "Yeah right." said Campbell before turning to face Ms. Washington.

Campbell begins, "Hello ma'am, I'm Detective Campbell, and this is my partner, Detective Brooks and we have been assigned to your son's shooting. What's your name?" Trembling she responded, "Sharon Washington." Deuce's mother tried to speak clearly. "How are you holding up?" asked Campbell. "We haven't heard anything yet, about Cliff's condition." Sharon responded ringing her hands together frantically.

Seeing the agony on the woman's face Campbell turned to her partner and said, "Brooks, see if you can get some info on her son's condition." "I'm on it." answered Brooks before turning to walk to the nurse's station. "Ms. Washington, I must let you know that time is of the essence and details are important, do you know of any problems your son had with anybody?" asked Campbell.

"Not at all... everybody like's Cliff... I don't know why this happened to my baby... I just want him to be okay."
"Are those his friends?"
"Yes." Ms. Washington nods her heads staring over at Allante', Melvo, Lump and Ru-boi. Campbell nods, hastily excuses herself and walks over to the boys. "Are you all friends, of Clifton Washington?" asked Campbell. She received no response from the

crew. "What are your names?" Melvo responded, "Do I have to answer that?"

"Yes."

"Melvin Foster."

"And yours?"

"Myron Armstrong."

"And you?"

"Derrick Jackson."

"And what's your name?"

"Allante' Light."

"Do you box?"

"Yeah."

"Yeah, I saw your fight at Cobo over the weekend… do y'all know who shot Clifton?" Lump answered, "Nawl, we lost just like you and we trying to find answers too." Campbell onced them all over before saying, "Well just leave that to us. Don't take matters into your own hands…"

She places her pad back into her pocket after writing their names down. She then stares deeply into Allante's eyes, "You'll be a World Champion one day if you stick with it.", complimented Campbell before turning to walk back over to Ms. Washington and her kids. Melvo said to the crew, "Man let's get out of here." They all walk out of the emergency room door. Outside Melvo began, "Fool, that police bitch ass was fat as shit." Lump added, "she seem like she was on your dick Alla." "Man, I ain't----

Gunshots suddenly erupt before they could take another step. The four of them instantly hit the ground. The green Impala skirted away out of the parking lot, getting up Melvo notices that Lump isn't moving. "Lump!" he shouts at his brother. Several people are running and screaming, Allante' rushes over to Lump's body. Blood is leaking out of Lump's left side and leg. "HE HIT! HEY! HEY!"

Ru-boi runs back into the hospital where he shouts for help. Melvo and Allante' pick up Lump's body, carrying him into the hospital. Blood is smearing their clothes. Nurses run to their aid to assist with Lump. A male doctor rushes up with a gurney and he places Lump's body on top of it. Detectives Campbell and Brooks rush up to the scene in the emergency lobby. Campbell stares at Lump's body and then to the two boys' bloody clothes.

"There were gunshots outside and... She pauses upon noticing a by-stander, "It came from a car but I couldn't see it... I just heard it speed off..." Campbell began, "Mr. Light--- "I didn't see the car. I heard shots and I ducked. We looked up and Lump was shot. That's all I know." answered Allante' cutting her off before she could finish. "What about you two?" asked Campbell. "We ain't see nothing either." answered Melvo and Ru-boi in unison. Brooks cuts in, "Look we want whoever is doing this, don't you guys want to help us?" Rushing up

on him in anger, Melvo yelled in Brooks face "My brother just got shot. Get the fuck out my face!" Campbell stepped between them, "Oh, I didn't know. Y'all don't have the same last name."
"Nawl, but he still my brother!"

Lump has already been rushed into the emergency room. Allante' looks over at Melvo before telling Ru-boi, "Come on Mo, I need to holla at you." Allante' turns back to Melvo, "Melvo call your mother, me and Ru-boi going back to the hood." Melvo immediately pulls out his cell phone and calls his mother to give her the sad news. Allante' and Ru-boi walk hurriedly out of the hospital and Detective Campbell sets out to follow them.

Allante pulls out his cell phone calling Heather. "Hey, Lump got shot!" "Oh my God! Are you alright? Where are you?" she asked frantically. "Somebody shot at us when we came out the hospital. Everybody was just standing on the sidewalk. Look, call Keisha and let her know. Tell Bree to come up here and wait with Melvo. I'm leaving the hospital now."
"What are you going to do?" asked Heather.
"I'm going back around my way."
"Allante' please be careful."
"Man, I'mma bout to murder some shit." Allante' gets into the passenger seat of Ru-boi's jaguar and

they leave the parking lot unaware that Detective Campbell is trailing them from a distance.

"Mo, its got to be them niggas from the movies, I saw the car, it was a green Chevy Impala. I know you got niggas over there that you serve and niggas over there that you fuck with, but I'mma bout to shoot that whole motherfucking neighborhood up if I can't find out who did this shit!" said Allante'.

"Homey, the niggas I fuck with over there they don't give a fuck about them fools over there. They live over there but that's it. You know where I stand. Fuck the money right now, I'm on some murder shit too homey. I'm about to make some calls and find out who got a green Chevy Impala." answered Ru-boi.

"Hey Ru-boi, that bitch following us Slim." said Allante' noticing Campbell in the distance. "Who?" Smirking he responds, "That detective bitch. Look, don't go back around that way. Go over on the eastside, we gon drive this bitch all over the city, until she get the hint that we ain't no dumb motherfuckers. Go ahead and call your peoples."
Allante reclines in the passenger seat with his eyes glued to the side mirror. Observing the Ford Taurus following them at a distance of four cars back, Allante's cell phone begins ringing. If it had been anyone else he wouldn't have given a second

thought to not answer the phone right now. He answers while keeping his eye glued to Campbell car. Pressing the speakerphone button Allante' answers, "What's up?" There was a brief pause before Heather asked him, "Where are you?"

"I'm taking care of some shit. What's up?"

"I'm on my way over to the hospital, I took Josh over to my mother's house, I'm about five minutes away from the hospital now."

"Let me know what's up with Lump and Deuce when you get there but when you leave go stay at your mother's house until I come and get you."

"Okay I love you, please be careful."

He ended the call.

ROSELAWN STREET

Sam said to his friends, "Man, I knew them niggas would be at the hospital." His brother Sunny responded, "This shit just beginning Sam." nodding his head. "Man, I don't give a fuck about them niggas or what they think they gon do. Its whatever!" said Sam. Kevin added, "Dawg be ready them niggas killers just be ready cause they gon come back" Sam snapped, "Man y'all keep talking about them nigga like y'all scared of them."

Odell then said, "Nawl, but we getting in some shit we ain't never been in before. You act like this shit is cool, this ain't no movie shit Sam. We out shooting niggas and best believe it Mo, they gon shoot back!"

DETECTIVE CAMPBELL
IN HER TAURUS

"Where in the hell are they going?" Campbell mumbled to herself. Her cell phone begins ringing. "Campbell speaking."
"Are you tired?"
"Excuse me!"
"Are you tired of following us? What you think we blind? Did we shoot Myron? Did we shoot Clifton? Why are you following us?"
"Who is this?"
"If this is Detective work, y'all are weak ass shit…" Allante' gave her the dial tone before she could respond. He watched her turn off on the street behind them. Allante' turns to Ru-boi, "That bitch gon Slim, go ahead over to the way."
"Got you homey." answered Ru-boi.

Detective Campbell is back on her cell phone, "Brooks, yeah they spotted me. I'm on my way back to the hospital. I need you to look at the hospital parking lot surveillance video and see if you can get the license plate number off the get-away-car, as well as see is there any shot of the shooter." Brooks replied, "The press is here." "Great; this is going to be a complete shit show starring us! Yelled Campbell." Nodding his head Brooks agreed. "I can hear that shit coming from the Captain now. We got to find these guys and try to contain this shit. Get the surveillance footage ASAP... I'll be there in about twenty minutes. We need to catch a break!"

RU-BOI'S JAG

"GOT IT HOMEY. I KNOW WHOSE CAR IT IS! Them niggas is dumb as shit mannnn they used they own car. The nigga who owns it lives on Roselawn." said Ru-boi after ending his phone call. "Drive over there and let's see if we see the car. I want to get this nigga tonight, I want to crush this motherfucker. If his car there, I got a plan to get'em." said Allante'.

SINAI HOSPITAL

"He got hit pretty bad. I don't understand this shit. He is lying on a fucking table! And they don't know if he's going to live!" said Keisha. Heather places her arm around her girlfriend. "We got to pray that Lump and Deuce come out of this okay. I can't believe that Alesha is dead." said Heather. Bree cut in, "Is all this shit because of what happened at the movies the other night?" Heather rolled her eyes at Bree, "Bitch keep your voice down... Listen, don't you talk to anybody about the other night. I don't care if bitches are out here gossiping, you don't say shit. Keep your mouth shut and act like you don't know what they are talking about... just let them handle it I'm talking about all of it and the boys. When Melvo be buying you shit it's all good. Well, this is the other side of it Bree. If you hear motherfuckers saying their names in this shit about the movie, let me know, and let me know who it is.", Bree responded weakly, "Okay Heather."

BROOKS ON HIS CELLULAR PHONE

"The car is registered to a Samuel Brisbron. He lives at 1824 Roselawn Street. He has a brother named Sunny Brisborn."
"Okay, get a car over there. I want him picked up." answered Campbell. "The surveillance shows three males, two shooters and one driver."
"Probably the brothers and a friend. Pick up Samuel and let's see if we can get him to talk."

1824 ROSELAWN STREET

"What's your name?" asked Allante'.
"Red." The man reeked of liquor and stale smoke.
"Okay Red, just go up to the door and ask for Sam. Here, this $500.00; that's all you gotta do."
"Alright!" Red's bloodshot eyes light up like a Christmas tree. Allante' and Red get out of the stolen mini-van, Ru-boi remains sitting behind the steering wheel. Moments later, Red is ringing the door bell and Allante' is hiding low behind a bush located at the front of the house. The front door opens and an elderly black woman with salt and pepper gray hair wearing a housedress stands before

139

Red. "Is Sam home?" Red spoke as clear as he could. "Hold on a minute dear…. Sam!"
She closed the door opening again, Sam now stood there, "Who are you?"

Allante' raises up from behind the bush moving swiftly with his mask pulled down over his face, his gun up and trained to shoot Sam dead in the face. Allante' squeezes the trigger releasing a succession of shots, blood splatters everywhere. As soon as Sam's body hit the ground, Allante' began shooting Red all in his face dropping him dead right beside Sam's body.

Brain matter and blood stain the brick walls of the once quiet home. Allante' dashes back up to the mini-van, Ru-boi already has the van in gear and once Allante's has his full body inside of the van, Ru-boi mashes the gas. Meanwhile the elderly woman has ran back up to her front door upon seeing Sam and the other dead victim she screams, "OH NO!!! OH NO!!!"

Her body collapses on the floor realizing that her son's life has ended, his blood and brains splattered all over the walls and porch. Kneeling down, she picks her son's upper body in her arms. Two twenty plus year old men rush to her side. Shocked at what their eye are seeing, they both bow their heads and tears begin rolling uncontrollably down their faces as Samuel Brisborn is another dead body, with more soon to follow.

IN THE MINI-VAN

"Mo, let's get rid of this joint! Look, I bet that police car going over there now." said Allante'. "You a motherfucker homey." said Ru-boi in response. "I'mma kill all them niggas. I'mma call and check on Lump and Deuce. We got to change and get rid of this van and go back up to the hospital. "Bet!"

SINAI HOSPITAL

"Shit! Shit! Shit!" said Detective Campbell hanging up her cell phone. "They killed Samuel Brisborn... They just fucking killed Samuel Brisborn." said Campbell to Brooks. "Who Campbell?"
"It was Allante' Light, and Derrick Jackson. I was following them, and they spotted my tag. One of them even called my damn cell phone to tell me just that!"
"How?"
"I gave them my card when I talked to them in the emergency hallway."
"Check the number on caller I.D. . ." Brooks said with confidence as if he'd solved the whole case. "I know it was a throw-away-phone, they're not stupid." Campbell rolled her eyes.

"Well, we don't have no proof that it was them then." Campbell stared in aggravation.
"They'll make a mistake… just give it time."
A few seconds later Allante' and Ru-boi walk back into the emergency room waiting area.

Campbell spots them and she makes a b-line straight towards them. "I know it was you!" yelled Campbell. "Me what?" responded Allante' calmly to Campbell. "Yeahhh you can play ignorant all you want. Where were you at 8:30 tonight?" Heather stepped up, "Don't answer her!" Campbell looks a Heather, "Young lady, please step back."

Standing firmly between them, "Lady he's only sixteen, ain't you supposed to have a parent present when you talk to him?" asked Heather. Campbell turns back to Allante', "You have a future Allante', don't throw it away." Campbell locks eyes with Allante'. "I still have a future." He stared coldly. "Okay, whatever you say." Campbell then turns, walking away.

Heather and Allante' then walk over to Lump's mother whose standing beside Melvo. One of Allante's best friends as well as a friend and partner in crime now lay in this same hospital that they rocked two young men to sleep in earlier in the month. Life has many twist and turns, but very few people can connect the dots.

WEST OUTER DRIVE

"Unc, Lump got shot and my boy Deuce got shot earlier today. Man, I'm mad as shit." Allante' is spitting into the speaker of his cell phone. "Calm down… people make mistakes when they move off of their emotions. You got to rise above your emotions in the face of decisions. What you do doesn't just affect you Allante'…

Remember you got people following your move, so what happens to them falls on your shoulders and it's only if you move right that you can win on all sides. Learn the lesson from all the dudes who ran these same streets before you. I don't know if there is a such thing as mastering the game, but you can master your emotions. Then, I guarantee no matter what you face, you can overcome it. Listen, I need to talk to you so come and see me tomorrow morning..."
"Okay Unc, I'll be there." said Allante' ending his phone call with T.

In the master bedroom, Heather is inside of the bathroom sitting on the toilet with her panties down, hands between her legs as the warm urine hits the stick. Heather bounces her legs up and down waiting anxiously looking down to see the positive sign on the pregnancy test. This is the second test that she has taken.

In her mind and heart, this is news that she will welcome because she is filled with a seed that will reflect the young man that she loves. "How would she tell him? What would be his response? "I'm going to play a part in changing his life and I'm going to love him no matter what." Heather said to herself.

6:30 A.M
THE NEXT MORNING

Heather wakes up in the bed as Allante' comes walking out of the shower. "I got to go make a run. I'm going to come back around 8:30 to pick you up." said Allante'. "Okay, I'll be ready." Sitting up on the bed she continued, "I need to talk to you about something..."

Turning to face her he began, "What's wrong?" Heather's facial expression began to worry him. "Nothing, I think it's good news, depending on how you feel..."
"Tell me what's up girl."
"I'm pregnant...." She notices that his facial expression has lightened with a glow, and she's immediately relieved seeing his smirk. "Are we good?" Heather asked with a trembling voice. "You just made me happy azz shit!"

The moment those words left his mouth she began crying tears of joy. "Aye, why you crying?

"Be-because I- I don't, wan want you to be mad at me." Heather tried to talk between her tears. Sitting down beside her, he asks, "Mad for what?" Holding her closer to him now, he continued, "Look at me, I been putting my dick in you, and cumming in you. I put a baby in you, I wanted you to have my baby. You're the only thing I did right Heather. I got you..."

He gently wipes the tears that are falling from her eyes away from off of her face. "You're already on your way. This house is paid for, you got a bank account, you're ready to graduate both High School and Cosmetology School then to top it all off you got a plan. It's not even about me. I grew from your presence in my life, then I earned my place.

Have I taught you anything? Have you learned from me? That's what's important Shorty. I'm happy as shit right now, and I love the fuck out of you..." Allante' then gently rolls his body over on top of her planting soft kisses all over her face. As they laid there holding one another time seemed to be standing still.

INSIDE OF THE RANGE ROVER

"What's up Mo, what's the word?" asked Allante'. "He ain't woke up yet but they got the slug out, so it's up to him... he got to fight. Deuce looking okay, he was woke but now he just went to

145

sleep.   They don't know how long he gon be in here. Where you at?" asked Melvo on the other end of the cell phone. "I'm on my way over T's house, me and Ru-boi. He said he needed to holla at me about something, then we on our way up there. We'll switch up so y'all can go get some rest. I'll see y'all in a few." ended Allante'.

T's HOUSE

"How are the boys doing?" asked T. "It's up to then now Unc, they out of surgery, so now is the fight for them." answered Allante'."
"I hope they pull through."
"They gone pull through."
"Listen, I got word that some Mexican trying to find information about a stash house robbery that happened a couple months ago. They say one of the people who got killed is related to a major plug. The Mexicans are hunting..."

"We hunters too Unc." Allante' spoke sternly. " These ain't kids Allante'… and they kill families, animals and whatever else to make their point." Allante' became enraged at T's disposition. "Unc, I'm a wolf! A wolf will bite his own leg off to get out of a trap. Point me in the right direction and I'mma take care of it." T smiles from ear to ear, "You got heart just like your father. Look, we can send a message that we ain't to be fucked with either but I'mma have to work it out first. I'm a part of it now. Be ready..."

"I'm always ready. An owl can spin his head all the way around his neck… 360 degrees. He ain't missing nothing and if I can help it, neither am I.

What about the other thing we did?" asked Allante'. "They ain't got no clue about y'all… and they scared to death." T assured Allante'. "Alright bet, we out, we headed up to the hospital. I'll drop that last joint off to you tomorrow. "That ain't even been on my mind."

"Okay! Hey, I got a young dude I want to introduce you to. I really like him and I want you to meet him." Allante' rubbed his hands together nodding his head. "Okay Unc, just call me when you ready we'll come… we out… come on Ruboi."

HOMOCIDE/ROBBERY UNIT

"Campbell, Dearborn police left a message on our phone that might be interesting to you." said Brooks. What is it about…do you know?"
"They had a drug robbery a few days ago."
"What makes that interesting for us?"
"The victims were killed with a nail gun to the face."
"Any witnesses?"
"I don't know."
"Well do a follow up and let me know what you come up with. We got all these bodies and shootings yet nobody has seen anything… Ain't no

perfect case or criminal but clearly we're missing something."

ON THE WAY TO SINIA HOSPITAL

"Homey y'all been putting in a lot of work and basically, I been a get-away driver, I'm trying to get my dick wet. I got a way to chop this up so we can move on." said Ru-boi. "What's up?" asked Allante'.

"They got to bury that nigga that you just killed and I don't give a fuck about his family cause we at war. I know them other niggas gone be there. We can get them niggas at the wake."
"It's probably gone be a lot of police at that joint."
"I'm hip, but I gotta plan about that too."
"What is it?"
"We can......."

SINIA HOSPITAL

Heather hugs Keisha as she walks in the room where Lump lays unconscious. Mrs. Armstrong and Melvo fill the other chairs in the room. "I stopped and got some food because I though y'all might be hungry." said Heather. "Thank you, baby, but I can't eat right now; I don't have an appetite." said Mrs. Armstrong. "I'm hungry as shit, excuse me Ma. I'm hungry, what you got?" Melvo grabbed the bags from Heather's hands. "I got some eggs, sausage, pancakes, and oh I got some donuts. Has Lump woke up at all?" Heather scanned the room for a response. "He moved a little, but he ain't open his eyes yet." said Keisha. "Ru-boi and Allante' should be here shortly, he had to go make a run." With his mouth stuffed, "He called me, I know what's up. I'mma walk down and check on Deuce, I'll be back."

Tears began falling down from Keisha's eyes. Heather hugs her girlfriend to comfort her. Heather turned to look at Keisha. "You stayed all night?" noticing she's wearing the same clothes as the day before. "Yeah, this nigga been fucking me so long now, I go where the dick go."
Both girls have a brief moment of laughter breaking the somber tone in the room.

"I don't know when this is going to end but we got to stick with them." said Heather. "Girl, I ain't going nowhere. I don't know about Bree scared ass, but...Bree walked into the room with a bag of food in her hands. "Bree what?" asked Bree. "I just ain't know if you was going to stick around." said Keisha. "I didn't come up like y'all, so don't know what to say and what not to say. But I love y'all, and I think I love Melvo so I'm here." "Alright girl, we got you." said Heather. The three girls hugged while continuing to talk.

IN ALLANTE'S RANGE

The cell phone begins ringing. My Favorite Girl appears on the Caller ID, "Hey Ma" answered Allante'. "Your school called and said you've missed a couple days in a row." Her tone was laced with concern. "Lump got shot and another friend did too. I'm on my way back up to the hospital."
"How are they?"
"Lump ain't woke up yet, Deuce my other friend woke up yesterday."
"Oh my God! You be careful."
"Alright Ma. Listen Ma, I got three classes left. I don't even have a full schedule so I don't know why they even called you but I go to school and I'm going to graduate so don't you even worry about that. I know what it means to you."
"Okay baby. I love you. Give my regards to Lump and Melvo's mother. I know how close y'all are."
"Alright ma, I love you, bye."

HOSPITAL ROOM

Allante' and Ru-boi walk into the hospital room. Allante' walks straight over to Mrs.' Armstrong giving her a tight hug and kiss on the cheek. He then walks over to Melvo dapping him up. He looks at the girls, pride fills his heart seeing that they are sticking it out with them. Allante' makes a mental note. "When drama, comes very few stick around." The circle the youngsters have forged a special bond. Grown men could learn a lot from this young group.

Loyalty doesn't exist anymore. The truth is, it never did. It was always rare. The streets only love you when you're up. It only pays tribute to the stars while it swallows up so many un-remembered, leaving in its path so many broken-hearted mothers, sisters and brothers. The streets don't love nobody...and sadly they never will. They suck life out of our communities and swallow up the promise of generations.

"Mrs. Armstrong, you and Melvo go get some rest. We got him, if anything changes, I'll call y'all ASAP." said Allante'. "Come on Ma." said Melvo. "Thank you, baby. I'll go home and take a shower and I'll come back later." answered Mrs. Armstrong. "Mo, on my life, we got'em." Allante' said to Melvo. "I know, I know mane." said Melvo. "Ru-boi came up with a plan for the other niggas. We gone cook that beef." Melvo looked in the faces of his friends, "I want to murder them niggas." Ru-boi flashed a devilish grin, "They gone be talking about this one homey."

"We out man; I'll holler at y'all when I come back." said Melvo walking out of the room with his mother. We getting ready to tell Deuce mother to go home and get some rest too. Allante' stared at the girls. "Y'all go to school man." At the same time, all of the girls, began, "But we wanna...

"Look, y'all go to school, we got Lump and Deuce. Y'all come back after school. I want to know what niggas is saying. We need y'all to be our second set of eyes and ears. But in order to do that y'all gotta go to school. Y'all got classes, y'all gotta take to graduate." said Allante' looking at Heather. He continued, "If I need you, I'll call you."

"Come on y'all let's go." said Heather. Allante' takes hold of Heather's arm and their eyes lock. "Don't tell nobody about the baby yet. I don't want nobody knowing until I clean this shit up." He said only loud enough for Heather to hear. "Okay." Allante' reached inside of his pocket. "Here, this is my lawyer's card. If I ever get into shit where they lock me up, call him ASAP. If the police ever pull up on you, call him, re represents you too."

"Okay, I love you. I'll see you when I finish Cosmetology school. Josh going to stay over my mother's house again. You need me to do anything else?"

"You know what, you're pretty as shit."
Heather smiles hugging Allante'. "Come on
bitches we gotta go. Keisha, I got to take your ass
home so you can change." They talk as they walk
out of the door.

INKSTER, MICHIGAN

"I don't think the shit going on over there
has anything to do with drugs Joker. From what I
heard, it started over a fight." Responded Joker.
"We got a partner over there whose looking into it,
if he comes up with names I'll get back to you. It's
not like we have a community over there. We stick
out. We can't just go up in there." said P-L-O.
"If you don't bring me somebody, he's talking
about killing families. Ours..."
"Okay, I'll keep trying, we don't have a choice."

MONICA STREET

Detective Campbell knocks on the door of
Deborah Light's house. Deborah answered the
door… "Hello, my name is Detective Campbell."
"Did something happen to my son?"
"No! Oh, I'm sorry, no nothing has happened to
Allante', can I come in?" Deborah opens the door
allowing Campbell to come in. "I'm investigating
the shootings of Clifton Washington, and Myron
Armstrong, and the murder of Samuel Brisborn, as
well as other multiple homicides."

"What does this have to do with Allante'?
"I'm trying to figure out if it has anything to do with Allante'." "Well, we need to end this conversation. I don't have anything else to say." Both women head back towards the front door. "Your son is a boxing genius with exceptional talent."

Campbell searched Deborah's face for a sign of concern or worry… she came up with nothing. "That he is. Have a good day Ms. Campbell." After closing the door, Deborah pulls out her cell phone speed dialing Allante'. "Call me as soon as you get this."

LUMP'S HOSPITAL ROOM

Sitting in the hospital room next to Lump's bed, Allante' looks at Lump. Lump's eyes open. Lump groans out in pain. "Don't try to move man."
"Mane, my shit fucked fool." Allante' begins laughing relieved that his friend is conscious. "Man, I'm just glad you woke."
"I slipped."
"Fuck nawl, you just got shot. You ain't slip. I'mma call your mother and Melvo. Deuce already woke.

Aye Mo, you a ugly nigga when you sleep and yo breath stank like shit!" Allante' leaned over laughing til his stomach hurts. "Fuck you nigga."

154

Lump smiles weakly before closing his eyes. The good news gives Allante' much needed energy. Murder, murder, murder...

FOUR DAY'S LATER
SWANSONS FUNERAL HOME
6 MILE & HUBBELL

Detectives Campbell and Brooks sit in the Ford Taurus, across the street from the funeral home. "Yeah, it should be almost over, let's just wait a couple more minutes." responded Campbell.

The sounds of dirt bikes, approaching the funeral home coming from down the street can be heard before the five dirt bikes stop in front of the funeral home popping wheelies, doing donuts in the middle of the street. The dirt bikes distract the attention of the two detectives.

Melvo, Allante', and Ru-boi slide unnoticed into the funeral home. Ski masks pulled down over their faces, all black clothing on, they all run up to the front of the funeral home and unload a succession of rounds on the three would be gangsters who had gotten in too deep with the wrong young lions. "Any of you brave ass motherfuckers move, murder, murder! Murder! Don't be a hero!" shouted Ru-boi. Melvo runs up to Sunny Brisborn's limp body, placing two more slugs into his face. "Let's go!" said Allante'.

As easily as they went in, they made it out. The noise of the dirt bikes covered the gunshots and the two detectives never heard a sound coming from inside of the funeral home. The three young lions disappeared around the side of the funeral home, and the dirt bikes rode off. Ru-boi was right, the streets would be talking about this for a long time to come.

Glorifying murder is easy, until it comes to your family's door. The streets will talk, but the families of the deceased will mourn.

LUMPS HOSPITAL ROOM

"That shit was sweet." said Melvo. "All you gotta do is give them young niggas some real live motivation and they gon cut up homey." said Ru-boi. "The police gon be mad as shit Mo. That bitch and her partner were sitting right across the street from that joint. This Ru-boi shit. You a monster Slim." responded Allante'. Ru-boi smiles, "Nawl, y'all niggas is monsters."

Deuce is sitting in the chair with his hospital gown on. Deuce began, "I ain't even get a chance to be a part of that shit." They all laughed at him. "Nigga you ain't superman, just get better. We cooked that beef." answered Allante'.

156

WEST OUTER DRIVE

Pulling up in front of his house, Allante' gets out of his Range walking to the back of his S.U.V. Pulling out a big box. He then walks to the door carrying the large box, putting the box down only to unlock the door, picking it back up going inside. Closing the door with his foot, he turns around to see Heather and Keisha sitting in the living room on the sofa as he walks into the living room carrying the box.

"What's up Alla?" greets Keisha. "Bae, what's in the box?" asked Heather. "What box?" "Boy stop playing." Josh walks over to sit beside the box when Allante' opens it up. "Oh my God!" said Heather. Two blue and white pit bull puppies poke their heads up out of the box. "They're so beautiful!" said Heather. "They bad as shit."

"These some bad lil mufuckas." Josh claps his hands at the puppies. The puppies are trying to jump out of the box. "Heather, I'm about to go. Shit, that nigga better get me some puppies when he get out of that damn hospital." Said Keisha. "You know what you got to do. You got to eat that dick up." Said Allante'. "Boy bye!" "Nawl, all jokes aside. Thank you for being there for Lump, I ain't going to forget it." "You alright Allante', you treat my girl good as shit. From day one you been real. I'mma hold

Lump down, you ain't gotta worry about that. That nigga owe me. This pussy ain't free. See y'all later." The sound of Escape the R&B group's song, "Softest Place on Earth," is playing in the bedroom on the music system. Not long after Keisha left, Heather put Josh to sleep, so she could have some time alone with Allante'.

They both are already undressed, Allante' is laying in the bed on his back. Heather straddles his waist, lowering herself onto his rock-hard dick. As she is facing him, rocking her pussy back and forth slowly, Allante' grabs a hold of her thick hips. "Damn, your pussy hot and wet as this pregnant pussy now." She winds her hips in a circular motion, whipping it after every rotation, looking for Allante's face, as she gives him all her love riding him.

Her young brown nipple become erect, and her sexual nature goes into overdrive. In and out, his dick disappears as she takes more and more of him inside of her. Heather stopped, she moaned out, "I want, you to see it." She gets up, turning around squatting her pussy and ass inches away from his face before sitting in reverse position onto his long dick.

Leaning forward, she purposely allows him to see the sight of his dick going in and out of her tight wet pussy, disappearing inside of her before coming out wet and slick. Poking her ass out, Allante' sticks his thumb inside of her ass-hole. Unable to see her face, Heather smirks. Allante' smiles knowing that she didn't like him sticking his finger into her butt. She continues to ride him reverse cowgirl before leaning back wiggling her pussy on his hard dick. As her body heats up, the rush comes and she loses control.

Her body is shaking, Allante' can feel the warm rush as she cums all over his dick. He grits his teeth, unable to control it anymore, he groans, "I'm cumming." She smiles knowing that she just broke him down. Between them they know, it's always about who's going to break first. Pregnant pussy proved to be too much for the young lion. Little did Heather know, she just has this effect on him. She's in a class of her own. She would know true love, one of very few women who would state that truth.

NORTH WESTERN HIGH SCHOOL

In class the next day, Allante's phone begins vibrating. He sees his mother's phone number on the Caller I.D. again. Five times she called, and five times he has avoided. He answers the phone knowing what's about to take place already. "Hello?"
"So, you just not answering my calls?"
"I don't want to be lectured Ma."

"I wasn't going to lecture you. I was trying to tell you that your brothers wanted to see you."
Hit with a sting, Allante' replies, "I'll be over there after practice, I'm in class right now so I can't talk." Allante' spoke in a low whisper. "I'll see you later on." She ended the call.

LATER ON

Detective Campbell's car is parked next to Allante's Range Rover as he comes out of the school. She leans over the side of her car, as he walks to his Range. "It's consequences to this." Said Campbell. "Consequences to what?" "A lot of people have died and gotten hurt. When does it end Allante'?"

"I don't know what you're talking about." "Nobody saw your face, no fingerprints, no D.N.A. I know it was you and your boys. How many mothers are going to mourn because of you Allante'? How many sisters and brothers are going to lose a brother?"

"I lost a brother, sixteen years old. He was shot and killed by a police. UNARMED! How many going to die by police hands? You a police, you tell me. I know pain just like those mothers. Just like little sisters and little brothers. I am them. I'm a product of society, for better or for worse. I don't want to see no mother hurt, if her children get in the streets, and get swallowed up, tell her to look at their fathers. Where are they? We might be the bullet, but we are not the gun. That's the streets. The trigger person is society. When society fails to care, they pull the trigger. So, when ain't nobody getting murdered, how much time do you and your partner spend caring… Yeah, just what I thought. I ain't kill nobody and I don't know who did. Are we done? I got a lawyer, next time you want to talk with me, talk to him…"

1642 MONICA

"Where you been?" Asked Arraja.
"I got my own place now." Answered Allante'.
"Why we don't see you anymore?" Asked Andre.
"Ma put me out. She don't like the way I live."
What are you doing wrong?" Asked Andre.
"Well, I just don't live by Ma rules anymore, but that don't mean that y'all not supposed to. Whatever she tells y'all to do, I expect y'all to do it.

Changing the subject, he asked them, "How much money y'all got?" Anxiously they answered "We ain't got no money." Responded his brothers. "Listen, you always got to have money. Here, this is a $100.00 apiece. Don't tell Ma I gave it to you, I'mma give y'all some money every week, make sure y'all keep the house clean for Ma. Clean up after yourself."

"When we gone see you again?" Asked the brothers. "I'mma come get y'all one day and take y'all shopping, and y'all gone come spend the night over my house with me and Heather."
"We love you." His brothers hugged him tightly.
"I love y'all too. It's time for y'all to go to bed. I'll see y'all later."

SITTING IN THE LIVING ROOM

"That female detective came over here. What are you doing Allante'?" Asked his mother.
"Ma, I'm living my life, you put me out at sixteen years old. You think I'm not going to survive?"

"You came to my house driving a freaking $80,000.00-dollar S.U.V. Do you think I'm going to let the Federal government or the Department of Justice destroy everything that I have worked for my whole life? Am I supposed to not look out for my seven and eight-year-old children? I cannot control you, but they are my responsibility."

"I respect that. I'm good Ma." He said somberly. "I love you, you are my first born, but you can't live in my house doing wrong." She held his chin in her hand. "I don't want to put you in jeopardy, I told you I'm good Ma, and I honestly understand. Don't worry about me, I'mma be alright?"

Allante' stands up from the couch, walks over to his mother kissing her on her cheek. Before he could step away from their embrace she softly spoke these words into her son's ears and they pierced his soul. "You can seem to have everything to the world, but what's really important, money and material things can't replace."

DRIVING HOME

Allante' pulls out his cellular phone calling Lump to check on him and Deuce. "What's up Mo?" Lump answered wearily, "Ready to get out this muthafucka Mane." They both laughed. "You out tomorrow nigga." We gon get you right Mo. "Shit, I want to be out right now. I'm trying to blow Keisha back out." Lump lightly coughed. "Shorty been up there at the hospital every day man."

"Yeah, I'm hip fool. Mane, this shit crazy how we came up, I can't believe this shit mane. A nigga shot me." Allante' laughed hysterically telling him, "You gon need a lot of tattoos now Mo." Looking at the phone with a smirk, "Nigga, I already got a lot of tattoos." Allante' seemed to be laughing even harder! "Mannnn that weak ass shit you got." Knowing he was alone Lump briefly started to inspect his own body. "What's wrong with my tattoos?"

163

Even young lions in the bush face the danger of being prey. The gun is a motherfucker when it's in the hands of a determined killer. Yeah, anybody can pull a trigger, but every man ain't a killer. Fight for your life young nigga, fight...

Suddenly a car rams full speed into Allante's car. "What the f-
Gunshots begin ringing off, the sounds of high powered, AK47's sounding off. The mini-van rammed the right quarter panel of the Range causing it to spin left. Two Mexican men jump out of the mini-van opening fire through the passenger side of the Range.

The S.U.V is riddled with bullet holes. Cars are skirting off nearly running into one another, the two Mexicans jump back in their vehicle and mash out. The streets quickly become silent, the screaming sound of Lump's voice coming through Allante's phone, the smoke from the gun and the smell of the gun fire fill the atmosphere.

MOMENTS LATER

"He's lost too much fucking blood! Hold on young man. Don't try to talk, look at me! That's right, look at me! How fucking soon are we going to get there…? Hurry the fuck up! Son, look at me! Fight! Hurry the fuck up! Get that fucking I.V. working!" Said the EMT. Allante's eyes fade, everything goes black… The EMT's work frantically as Allante' goes into Cardiac Arrest. Only time and his strength to fight will tell if he survives.

SCENE 6:
THE PREY OF THE PRIDE

WEST OUTER DRIVE

Standing over the kitchen stove in booty shorts cooking seafood stir-fry, Heather looks over in the dining room. She begins smiling upon seeing Josh sitting on the carpet with the two puppies jumping up and down all around him. As her cell phone begins ringing, she stops to answer it.

Immediately tears begin to stream down her face uncontrollably as she bends down sitting in a fetal position with her back against the stove. The news just received from Lump is too much for the pregnant sixteen-year-old to bare. As sounds of her moans and uncontrollable cries fill the air, her one-and-a-half-year-old son notices the pain his mother is experiencing.

He quickly fumbles his way over to her. She grabs, holding him tightly with an embrace that only a mother can understand. As the young boy begins to cry in her arms, she gathers herself, standing up she turns off the stove. With Josh in her arms she runs upstairs, placing him down on the bed, she hurriedly dresses in sweat pants, and a pair of running shoes.

Picking Josh back up, she runs down the stairs to the front door, pausing to look at the puppies once more before making a mental note that she has to come back and get them. She opens and close the front door with Josh in her arms. Running to the Car, she takes off. Her destination 1642 Monica.

DEBORAH'S HOUSE

Heather pulls up to a stop in front of the house on Monica. She grabs Josh, and runs to the front door of the house with Josh. Knocking on the front door, she waits impatiently for an answer. Deborah Light opens the door, seeing the tears running down Heather's face, fear fills her heart.

"Where is he? Where is Allante'!?" Deborah demanded. Tears instantly stream down Deborah's face as she waits for Heather to speak. "I-I, do, don't know. Lu- Lump called me. He told me, he was talking to Allante' on the phone. He said he heard Allante's car crash, and a, a lot of gunshots. He said he kept calling Allante' name, and Alla, Allante' didn't answer. "Start calling the hospitals on your cellular phone! Where is my damn cell phone?" Said Deborah. Anxiously Deborah searches her home for her cell phone while Heather dials Information on her own cell phone to begin searching for Allante'.

Frantically calling the phone numbers of the hospitals that they received from information, Heather yells, "He's at Detroit receiving! They just brought him in, he's going into surgery in the Emergency room right now." Tears roll from Heather's eyes as she grabs Josh and heads out the door.

"He's lost a lot of blood and went into cardiac arrest. They said they don't know if he's going to make it." Said Heather. "Arraja! Andre! Let's go!" Shouted Deborah. The two brothers came rushing down the stairs. They all left heading downtown to Detroit Receiving Hospital located on St Antoine Avenue.

Dialing Lump's phone number, Heather gave him the information that Allante' has been shot, and the hospital that he's in. Heather also told him that she was riding there to the hospital now with Allante's mother and brothers and she would call him back once they make it there.

Hanging up the phone, Heather firmly places both of her hands on top of the steering wheel navigating between the cars in the way of her and her destination. Allante' needed her and no one is going to stop her from getting to him.

SINAI HOSPITAL

Dialing his brother cellular phone number, Lump gets out of his hospital bed looking for clothes to put on. "Bra, Alla got shot! Come get me!.... Fool, I was on the phone talking to him and it sounded like a car hit him. Then I heard shots like a AK.... Nigga come get me! Heather just called me and told me that he at Detroit Receiving...

When the shit happened, I called her and told her to get in touch with his mother. They together now, on their way down there. Look mane, call Ru-boi... I'm going over to Deuce room now... Mane fuck that! Fool, they don't know if he gonna make it. I'mma call T now and let him know what's up. Hurry up Melvo!"

WALKING DOWN TO DEUCE'S ROOM

Lump is dialing T's number on his phone. "Hello, Unc, mane they hit Alla. Unc they say they don't know if he's gone make it, he at Detroit Receiving. Heather and his mother on their way down there.... Nawl Melvo on his way to pick me up. He was by himself on the way home. Melvo calling Ru-boi, I'm going to Deuce room now. When Melvo get here we on our way down there. I'll see you down there." He ended the phone call. Walking into Deuce's room, the thought sets into Lump's mind that Allante' might not make it.

169

"Mane, they hit Alla." Said Lump. Shaking his head Deuce responded, "Nawl man. Nawl. Don't tell me that Lump. I don't want to hear that shit." "They hit his Range mane. I was on the phone with him. Heather found him at Detroit Receiving. Mane, they don't know if he gon make it. They hit my fuckin man! Melvo suppose to be on his way up here. Heather and his mother on their way down there."

"Help me get up, I got clothes over there, get my shit." Lump paced the floor in pain fueled with anger. "Ain't no more of them niggas out there, they all gone. This some other shit. I called T, and he's on his way down there. Whoever did this mane, I'mma kill everybody they love." "That's my muthafuckin nigga Mane. Ain't shit to talk about. Let's go, we might as well catch Melvo in the parking lot."

DETROIT RECEIVING

At Receiving Hospital, Heather, Mrs. Light and the boys rush into the hospital. As they run up to the information desk, Allante's mother takes control immediately "Excuse me! My son, Allante' Light was brought in here, shooting victim, sixteen years old, about 5'6, brown complexioned."

"Cathy! Go get Dr. Shaw. Ma'am, I believe he's being operated on right now. I just had one of our nurses go get one of our emergency room doctors to give you more information." Answered the head nurse. Dr. Shaw, a slim Indian Doctor, around forty years old approached the two women, hesitantly looking them into their worried eyes. "Hello. Are you the young man's mother that was brought in?" Dr. Shaw extended his hand. "Yes, his name is Allante', Allante' Light." "Is your name Mrs. Light?"

Dr. Shaw spoke in a low monotone voice. With her mouth trembling she said, "Yes." "Mrs. Light, Allante' has suffered a lot of trauma to his body. He's lost a lot of blood. While he was being transported he went into Cardiac arrest. His vital signs are weak. I can assure you that the Doctor's in the emergency room are doing the best work that they possible can." Heather cut in, "Is he going to make it?"

"It's too soon for us to know. Let me go inside and see what's going on, and as soon as I know something about our progress I will come to you. They have been working on him now for about forty-five minutes. Why don't you have a seat and I'll go back in the operating room."

Heather's shoulders sink in, tears begin flowing like a river from her eyes. Mrs. Light places her arms around her and Heather hugs her back tightly. Arraja, and Andre look at their mother before asking, "Ma, is Allante' going to be alright?" Mrs. Light squats getting to eye level with her sons'. "Allante' is in that room, and they're working on him. Now you know I'm not going to lie to you. Allante' is in real trouble, and he's going to have to fight. I need for you two to be strong. You know how your brother expects you two to fight for each other?" Nodding they answered "Yes." Smiling at her strong young sons, "Well, now we have to fight for him. We are going to pray to God that he gives Allante' strength to win over what he is fighting." She seemed to know exactly what to say to calm the storm inside of them. The boys once again tell their mom, "Okay." She hugs her sons.

After seeing Mrs. Light eloquently handle her sons in understanding of what was going on with their brother, Heather wiped her eyes and her face. She straightened her shoulders determined to represent Allante' with strength. The young lioness takes what she has learned from her young man and remembers that she is carrying his seed. The life that is growing in her womb will not be fed on sorrow and self-pity, but will feed on strength and courage.

In a moment of clarity, Heather finds her identity. Now is the time to rise, and represent what she knows Allante' saw inside of her. A THOROUGH LADY.

LUMP, MELVO, AND DEUCE

Lump, Melvo and Deuce entered the emergency room at Detroit Receiving looking as if they were about to murder someone. Walking through the busy front lobby, people immediately move out of their way as if they are parting the red sea. Seeing Mrs. Light, Heather, and Allante's little brothers, they make a b-line over to where they are seated and the question start to come.

"Where is he?" Asked Lump. Heather answered, "They're in their operating on him." "What they saying?" Asked Melvo. "He lost a lot of blood and went into Cardiac Arrest."
"So, what the fuck is they doing?" Asked Lump. "They're trying to save his life. Listen, he was shot multiple times in his right side, and chest. It was an assault rifle, and the bullets have ripped through his body. We don't know if he's going to make it." Said Mrs. Light.

Lump punches the wall with his fist out of pure anger. Mrs. Light began, "Myron, you have to calm down baby." Shaking his head violently with his fist balled up Lump continued with his rage filled rant. "Nawl, he in that room over there and I can't see what they doing. This shit ain't right, he ain't suppose to be in there." Heather then cut in, "Lump!" He gave her a menacing glare. "I don't want to hear that shit. If he don't make it, I'mma kill so many motherfuckers in this city, ain't nothing nobody can tell me!" Melvo sat in a chair staring at the floor. Looking up slowly, "When the last time the doctors came out here?" Asked Melvo. "About twenty minutes ago. He said they was doing all they can…

Somebody should be coming out to give us an update on what's going on. He's going to be alright. I know he is. We got to hold his mother down. Call your mother and tell her to come down here. I called Keisha and Bree also. They're on their way. Allante' needs our support right now, so that's what we are going to give him. Y'all are his best friends, right now we just gon be right here for him." Said Heather.

Seeing the group of people gathered around, and assuming that they are the young boy's family, the EMT walked over looking at Heather. "Excuse me, I brought a young man in here today who was driving a black Range Rover. Are you his family?" Asked the EMT. "Yes, he's my boyfriend."
"I want to talk to you about something in private." Stepping to the side, Heather, Lump, Melvo, and Deuce give the EMT man their full attention.

"Look, I'm not supposed to do this, When I went to check your boyfriend's body, he had a vest on, that vest saved his life because it took some of the force off of those rounds. He was hit pretty bad, but it could've been worst. The police have not arrived yet, so they don't know that we have it. If it disappears he can't be charged with being in possession of one." Heather answered, "I'll slide away and meet you outside." The man smiled and whispered, "Good girl." Heather turned to the guys, "Y'all go over there, and talk to Mrs. Light. I'll be right back."

Walking out of the emergency room entrance doors and into the area where the ambulances are parked, Heather meets with the EMT accepting the Bullet-proof vest that belonged to Allante'. Seeing his blood on the vest, Heather tightened up. Just as quickly she pulls herself back together. The EMT man looks at her, then he begins, "He told me to tell you to hold him down." "Excuse me?" Asked Heather her eyebrows wrinkling up. "While I was working on him, he told me to tell you to tell you to hold him down. He said for you to tell his brothers, Mexico."

"Okay. Thank you. Nobody will ever know what you gave me, or what you said to me." Said Heather looking around making sure no one was watching them. "He said that he loves you. He called you Beautiful." Heather begins smiling, laughing and crying all at the same time. Losing it, Heather walks away fast to put the vest inside the trunk under some new clothes. After she composed herself she went back into the emergency room.

Seeing her mother sitting beside Mrs. Light gives her more confidence. Turning to see her girlfriends walking into her direction strengthened her resolve that she could handle her business. As her girlfriends walked up and they all hugged, Heather told Lump, Melvo and Deuce that she needed to talk to them. Just as they stepped off to the side, Ru-boi came walking into the emergency room.

"Where the homey at?" Heather answered Ru-boi, "He's in the emergency room."
"How is he?" Lump answered, "We waiting to find out, they should be out in a minute." Heather spoke, "Listen, the EMT just told me that Allante' told me to tell his brothers, Mexico…." Lump and Melvo looked at one another, and Heather could see that they understood.

"I know tall know what he talking about." Said Heather. Melvo answered, "Yeah, he saying the Mexicans shot him up." Deuce cuts in, "Who the fuck is the Mexicans?" Lump answered, "Look we'll explain it to y'all later, but it don't matter, we getting ready to tear this motherfucking city up." "Whoever it is, I want all of them motherfuckers dead! He would do it for you." Said Heather in all sincerity. Looking at the ice in Heather's eyes. Lump and Melvo in that moment bonded with

Heather in a way that she would always have their respect and love. They knew that she loved Allante' for real, and the young lions knew that they had another member in their pride. A lioness, who would prove to be a force to be reckoned with in her on right. Heather would soon prove to them all that she is a reflection of her man. What Allante' saw in her would soon be revealed to them. When she loves, she loves hard. Little did she know, 'TRAILS ARE MADE TO BRING THE BEST OUT OF YOU."

Allante' saw it in her the first time they met. She was a star, and now she would shine. When the emergency room doors opened, the sixty-year-old something man who walked through the door had a strike of confidence, that could calm the most serve storm. Seeing T walk into the room, gave Lump and Melvo reassurance that nobody else but Heather could feel. That's because they knew him, and they knew that Allante' trusted him. When T walked up, they knew that they would get to the bottom of the situation, they all wanted to fuck somebody up for what they did to Allante'.

"Unc, the Mexicans did this shit." Lump enlightens T. "How is he?" Just as T asked the question, the Indian doctor came out of the O.R. Everyone gathered around Mrs. Light.

"Mrs. Light, Allante' has suffered major damage to his internal organs. His right lung has collapsed, and his shrapnel was lodged near his heart. We removed everything. We've done all we can. He's on a ventilation machine, he can't breathe on his own right now. These next couple of hours and days are going to be critical for him. If he can fight off the infection, he has a good chance of pulling through. I'm sorry, and I hope everything works out for your son." Said the doctor.

Heather started, "He knows how to fight. That's one thing can't nobody beat him in." "Young lady, I'm rooting for him to come through." The doctor tried to sound as optimistic as he could. "I know he's going to pull through." Heather knew that every reason in the world for Allante' to pull through was growing in her womb. He knew he was going to be a father, and she knew he wasn't going to leave her to raise their child on her own. Heather touches her stomach and thought to herself, 'He's going to fight for you.'

T pulled to the young lions to the side. "We can't talk about this here, but we can't all leave as well. My nephews are coming up here, so I'mma have one of them come up here and sit for a while, while we put what and who together to make a message that these motherfuckers will understand clearly. His jaw was clenched as he spoke, "I know what they understand." Ended T. Heather hugs Deborah after talking to the Doctor. They both notice the head nurse coming out of the operating room, heading in their direction. Heather began to speak as the nurse approached. "When can we see him, he needs to know we're here." With sadness in her eyes the nurse caringly responded, "Sweetheart, he's not conscious. I'm sorry, he's in pretty bad shape, but he fought through the surgery, he has a lot of spunk."

"He'll hear when I get to him, I need to see him." Said Heather.
"And who are you?"
I'm his...
"Family." Cut in Deborah.
"I want to see my child." The nurse looks for sympathy and understanding being a mother herself... "Only two of you can go in at a time. I want you to prepare yourself. It's going to be emotional." Deborah looks at her boys. "She and I are going in, as well as those two... His little brothers." Knowing that the young man's mother was not going to accept no for an answer, the nurse didn't put up a fight.

Heather, Deborah, and Allante's little brothers all entered Allante's room together. Immediately the somberness of the moment could be felt. The ambiance of the room was a dim light, multiple medical machine, sounds of beeping and the single bed with a young man laying stiff upon it with no signs of movement. Seeing Allante' in such a vulnerable state brought so much emotion to both Deborah and Heather, and Arraja and Andre immediately begin to cry for their big brother seeing him hooked up to so many machines.

As Heather began to slowly approach the bed, tears poured form her eyes. The love of her young life was right before her, and she need him to know that she was there with him. Softly touching his hand and running her fingertips up his arm, Heather bends her body over Allante's, leaning her pretty face over his. Whispering in his ear, "I'm here babe. I found you and I'm here." She wipes tears from her eyes.

Heather cleared her throat, "You have to wake up Allante', you can't stay sleep. I need you. You know what you told me, that you would always be here. I love you so much, please come back to me. Your son is going to need you to teach him things that I can't teach him. I'mma hold you down. You're my knight in shining armor. I love you." She bends lower, softly kissing him on his cheek. She turns to Deborah, stepping backwards so Deborah can come to the side of her son.

Stepping up to her son's side, Deborah touches his face. Her lips tremble looking into his helpless face she softly spoke, "You didn't even cry when you came into this world, you were such a smart baby. I know you can hear me Allante', you have to wake up. I can't lose you. I can't take that. Your brothers need you, and I have to tell you a secret that you can't tell them. You are my first love. When I held you in my arms for the first time, I know what love was. Fight son, we need you to fight."

Arraja, Andre, and Heather gather around Deborah and look upon Allante', as he quietly lays before them, while internally his body is fighting to over-come the trauma that has been afflicted upon him. The bandages around his head stem from the impact of the airbag when it was dispersed from the impact of the mini-van. He also suffered two broken ribs from the accident alone. Tubes are pumping oxygen through his mouth and nose helping him to breathe. The wounded young lion has never faced the magnitude of this challenge ever in a boxing ring.

Death is a motherfucker, and fighting him, even other angels come up short when they get in his path.

Knowing very well even without being told to do so that Heather was not going to leave his side, Deborah says to her, "Heather, I'mma go out here and let some of the others come in so they can see him. Don't leave his side." Eyes closed and tears still flowing Heather turns around slowly and says, "Mrs. Deborah. I'm pregnant. We just found out and he was so happy. He told me not to tell nobody yet, but he was so happy. I'm not leaving his side, you don't have to worry about that."

The two embrace, and the family increased in number. Even out of tragedy, families rise, and bonds are forged. Heather, and Deborah Light's bond would now be unbreakable. The young lioness, now sits in a position where she truly is the Queen on the throne.

EMERGENCY WAITING ROOM

When Deborah walked back into the waiting room, she saw Norma Armstrong. She smiled, and the two women embrace. Their children have been best friends for eleven years now, and the two women have become close as well. Deborah and Norma know that their sons are inseparable, so they both understand this would not go unanswered.

Heather's mother quickly enters the fold, and the three black women would be the backbone of this extended family like so many others have been from generation to generation. Black women have always been the backbone of the black community and they always will be.

Lump, and Melvo walk into the room where Heather sat by Allante's s side. The brothers looked at their best friend and without looking at his brother, Lump said, "I'm bout to call dad, this shit is bigger than us. We need to get dad, and Lewis up here." His brother immediately perked up at the thought. "This shit bout to turn up. Dad and Lewis be on some wild shit Lump. You know they like to play with them nail guns. I heard shit about them niggas shooting niggas in the nuts, nailing niggas to the wall like Jesus on a cross, cutting niggas dicks off, and blow torturing them like roasted hot dogs. Mane, them motherfuckers is crazy as shit." Responded Melvo.

"I want every motherfucker who had anything to do with this dead, I don't care how many of them it is. Find them and kill them motherfuckers. All of them." Said Heather.

OUTSIDE DETROIT RECEIVING HOSPITAL

The News Reporter is speaking, "Violence and Mayhem have once again struck the inner city. Hello, I'm Tina Dance, and tragedy has once again hit our beloved city as boxing phenom, Allante' Light was seemingly ambushed on the West Side of Detroit last night. Allante' is now on Life Support here. While reports of his S.U.V. being hit in the rear by a late year mini-van, witnesses say two Hispanic males jumped out of the mini-van and that a barrage of bullets riddled the S.U.V. driven by Allante'. Other questions have emerged, such as how is a sixteen-year-old driving an

$80,000.00-dollar Range Rover. The amount of carnage that has taken place over the last several months have now led for request of the Mayor and the Chief of Police to step down. With no arrest for the deaths of several young black males, so many black mothers are left to feel like their children are not valued in our society. Allante's shooting is bringing a light to a problem that many City Council don't want to deal with. While the prayers of the community are pouring out for this young boxing hopeful, countless more prayers are that the violence in the streets of Detroit and inner cities across the nation will cease, and the healing process can begin. I'm Tina Dance at Detroit Receiving Hospital."

Entering the hospital, Detective Campbell headed towards the emergency room nurse station. As she approached the station she noticed three older black women talking standing together. She recognizes Deborah Light. Looking a little further she noticed a group of young men accompanied by an older man talking. Taking a deep breath, Campbell approached the three women.

"Excuse me lady's. Mrs. Light, I'm sorry about the news of Allante', can I speak with you for a moment in private?" The other two lady's nod their heads at Deborah before stepping off.

"There is no good timing, for me to talk to you Mrs. Light, but I need to know, did Allante' talk to you about any problems that he had with anybody, or call you even recall anyone that he was upset with, maybe was it something he saw that may have put him in danger, that would cause somebody to want to kill him? Now before you answer, let me be clear, that was a hit. Whoever did that could try to come back and finish off the job. Allante' is still in danger, and so are you. Frankly, all of you are in danger."

"I only know my son to be a popular amateur boxer, and a typical teenager about to graduate from High School." Said Mrs. Light. "Mrs. Light, typical teenagers don't drive $80,000.00-dollar S.U.V's. Your son is into more than he can handle." Tilting her head Deborah sternly spoke, "Look, Allante' is in that room fighting for his life, I don't have the answers that you are looking for."

Campbell sensed she was in a losing battle, "If you had them, would you tell me?" Deborah stares at Detective Campbell with hate in her eyes. "I gave him life, and I will die to protect him. I have to go now." Deborah turns walking away. Campbell walks over to Brooks. "They're not going to help us, we are going to have to figure all of this out by ourselves."

Lump and Melvo walk out of the room Allante' is in. they stop at T, Ru-boi, and Deuce. Norma Armstrong called the two brothers to give them a word before they could leave. "Be careful, and make sure you come back to me in one piece. I know how much he means to y'all. Focus on what you got to do, we got this here." Melvo said "That's all I needed to hear Ma." She gently patted him on the shoulder, "You watch each other's back, and we'll worry about the rest later, I love y'all."

Walking over to the group, Lump pulled out his cellular phone, "I'm about to call down there to Memphis." Dialing the number, he waited for someone to answer. Lump said, "Hello… Who this…. Maria… What's up…? This Lump…Yeah I need to talk to my dad about something…I'll wait…Hello, dad..."

"What's up boy?" Asked B.G. on the other end of the phone line. "We need to see you." Lump answered purposely leaving the convo short.

"What's going on?"

"We need to see Lewis too."

"Say no more."

"A-S-A-P."

"On our way."

"Dad"

"Yeah."

"It's thick as shit."

"Lump, don't worry, we gon thin it out when we get there. Let me get off here, and get Lewis, we on our way, we'll be there in a few hours." Hanging up his cellular phone, Lump looked at Melvo and T. "My daddy on his way up here from Memphis with his partner Lewis. They say they'll be here in a few hours. My daddy run shit down there and they be putting in that work." T. nodded "Good, we need it to be loud and clear because that's all these Mexicans understand."
"Let me tell Heather we out."

Going back into the room, Melvo sees Allante's hand inside of Heather's hand. "We bout to roll out and put some shit together. Here, I want to give you this gun…" Heather opened up her Gucci backpack and pulled out a .40 caliber handgun. "Alla been taught me how to shoot. I ain't worried about nobody coming up in here, I got this. Melvo, we need to end this shit quick."
"I know how you feeling Heather. They're going to pay for this." Her eyes were almost swollen from crying, "They have too." Melvo left the room, leaving Deuce as male protection, as he, Lump, Ru-boi and T left the hospital.

MELVO'S 760

Riding over T's house in Melvo's 760, Lump leaned the passenger seat back a little, looking out the side-view mirror. "Melvo something ain't right about this shit." Lump pondered; "We don't sale drugs and that's the thing. He then continued, "Why would they come at us?" Melvo briefly took his eyes off of the road, "They wouldn't unless…" Lump nodded and said, "Somebody we know, out them on the lick we did."

"Only one person knew." Said Melvo.

"T!" The brother's said in unison.

"Damn fool, this bitch ass motherfucker." Said Lump.

"But why?"

"We bout to find out in a minute."

"He the reason Alla up in that room man."

"And he think he bout to cook us."

"Look mane, call him and tell him we got to make a stop and we'll be over his house in about a hour."

"Why?"

"Because you the only one who got a gun mane, we gotta go get some heat. And we got to come up with a plan to stall this nigga, until daddy get here. He'll know how to play this shit out. Call Ru-boi and put him on point too."

Melvo called T on his cell phone. He gave T a spill for the reason why they would be late. Lump got on his cell phone and called Heather telling her to be on point about T's nephew. The young pride of Lions would not be rocked to sleep again. "Keep your friends close and your enemies closer. Mane, we almost walked ourselves right into the fire." Said Lump. "Damn Alla's father suppose to be his man." Shaking his head in disbelief, "This is the worst kind of snake. He don't let you know he even there. When you finally see him it's too late. When daddy, and Lewis get to him, we gon get some answers." "I want to see this nigga torched in the worst way fool."

T'S HOUSE

"Look, I'm working on it now. I told you I'll deliver them too you. Just give me a little longer. Everything is coming along. Just have my money with you and the package we worked out. No, they don't have a clue. Just be easy, they'll be yours in a minute." T said into his phone before hanging up.

BACK AT THE HOSPITAL

Still needing the help of the hospital machines to breathe, Allante's body struggles to understand how to overcome the trauma that it is going through. Heather is still holding his hand. She lays her head on her own arm beginning to pray. "God, I know you can hear me. I know I don't always do what I'm supposed to do, but you're the only one who can help him. Please bring him through this. I need him to get through this God. We need him to get through this. I… Allante's hand begins twitching in her hand, she lifts her head up looking into his face. She can see his eyelids starting to twitch.

Wiping tears from her eyes with her hand, she straightens up in the chair. His eyes open up. She looks up to the ceiling smiling in disbelief. God has answered her prayer before she could finish getting the words out of her mouth. He squeezes her hand, she reaches to push the Nurses button for them to come. Saying "THANK YOU" to no one in particular, Heather now knew that God specialized in working miracles.

2 HOURS LATER
T'S HOUSE

"They told me they would be here in about a hour, and that was an hour ago, so they should be here any minute. Lump left the hospital without getting his medicine so they went to get some medicine for him." Ru-boi had laid the trap, and the boys plan. T would be very surprised soon that the young lions are several steps ahead of him. They called it baking him a cake. They were about to have a going away party. T would be sent out in style, and the city of Detroit would be talking about it for years to come. Young lions hunting, they don't call them Kings for nothing.

SCENE 7:
YOU CAN DANCE WITH THE DEVIL...
JUST BECAREFUL NOT TO STEP ON HIS TOES

DETROIT METRO AIRPORT

Waiting at the terminal, Lump's cell phone begins to ring. Looking at the number on the Caller I.D., he answers quickly. "Hello...What's up?" A smile appears on his face instantly. "That's what's up, hold him down... We'll be there when we finish taking care of this business. Hey, be on point..." Lump ended the call turning to Melvo. "Allante' opened his eyes. He went back to sleep, but he gon come through this shit." Lump said. "We gon give him something to smile about when we see him." said Melvo.

Coming through the terminal gate between the crowds of passengers, walked two black males in their mid-30's carrying Louis Vuitton travel bags. Lump bumps with his elbow as Melvo nodded his head in the direction of the crowd of people. Melvo smiled and the two brothers headed toward the two men. Lump began, "What's up daddy?" Pulling him in with a one-handed hug. "What's up lil nigga, what's going on?" Asked B.G. "What's up Uncle Lewis?" Said Lump. "What's up lil fool? What we up here for?" Responds Lewis. Melvo said, "We'll fill y'all in on the way to the house."

"We need to pick up some shit on the way. I need some rope, razor blades, duct-tape, a blow torch, and we need some gas. We'll figure out the rest of the shit we'll need." Said B.G. "Daddy we need to get this nigga now and make him talk so we'll know what all we facing." Said Lump. "Lump we been doing this shit before you was born, let's go mane. Talk while we walking." Answered B.G.

DETROIT RECEIVING HOSPITAL

Bernice Campbell sits in her Taurus, in the hospital parking lot trying to put together in her mind any type of pattern for the murders and shootings that have spread like wild fire on the west side of Detroit.

Starting with the murder by University of Detroit, the witness said there were three young black males. That crime was classified as a drug/robbery/murder. The murder weapon was a knife. The dealer sold weight in marijuana, and also cocaine. The second murders happened on Lilac. Three brutal murders, the victims were Mexicans. No doubt it was a Mexican drug stash house. The witnesses stated that they observed three young black males leave that house as well.

The first robbery, the victim was black, the second robbery the victims were Mexican. There was another robbery/murder in Dearborn, Michigan, where one woman, and two males were killed by nail guns. Those victims were Arabs, traces of heroin were found in the house. The motives of these murders are clear, drugs, and money...

Suddenly without an explanation the murders began to change. The one difference is that they don't appear to be about money anymore. These murders are believed to be neighborhood beefs. Two of her suspects in the neighborhood are shot, one believed to be shot by now a deceased rival, but the other suspect by Mexicans. Could it all be tied together about drugs and turf?

She puts her pad down, looking up she notices an off-duty officer walking into the hospital, he has on hospital scrubs. Being curious, she gets out of her vehicle walking back towards the hospital.

WEST Mc NICHOLS (6 Mile)

Driving down McNichols toward their house, Melvo stops at a red light. As the group of men and young men talk in the car, a gunshot is fired, and the rear glass back window is shattered out of the 760. All four men duck down, and Melvo floors the 760, mashing the gas, speeding through the red light.

"What the fuck!? Who the fuck is shooting at us fool?!" Shout's B.G. "It must be the Mexicans!" Lump yelled out. Lewis quickly yelled, "Give me a gun so I can bust back!" Melvo moves the 760 through traffic while Lewis fires shots through what use to be the back window. Turning down a side street, the gray mini-van that had been following them since the airport kept going. "How far are we from the house?" Asked B.G. "We right around the corner." Answers Lump. "Get us there, and then get me to this nigga T, we bout to cook this nigga. Fool you ready?" Asked B.G. "As a motherfucker!" Answers Lewis

DEQUINDRE STREET
1 HOUR 30 MINUTES LATER

Getting off of the phone, T turns to Ru-boi. "The move we have will only be good for a couple more hours. Where the hell are they?" Asked T. "I don't know." Answered Ru-boi. Just then Ru-boi's cell phone begins ringing. "Hold on Unc, it's Lump… Hello?" Ru-boi puts a little bit of distance between himself and T. "UN huh….Yeah…UN huh… Okay… I got you." Ru-boi ended the call. "They pulling up now." Said Ru-boi to T. Outside a car horn sounds off. Ru-boi walks to the window. T follows, unaware of the play that's about to happen… As T looks out the living room window, Ru-boi puts his desert Eagle to T's temple. "Bitch ass motherfucker! We looked up to you!" Gritted Ru-boi.

Pressing one button to dial the last incoming call on his cell phone, Ru-boi spoke with a disgust. "Yeah, I got'em. Come on in." Ru-boi said. Walking into the house, B.G told Lump to pull all of the curtains closed. Pulling his gun out from the back of his jeans, now inside of the house, B.G. walks up to T and smacks him in the back of his head with the gun. T's ear splits instantly and blood splatters everywhere. Grabbing his ear, T begins screaming.

"Wha-- what the fuck, y'all doing?!" Asked T. "Nigga, what you thought cause we was young we wasn't gon figure this shit out? Why? Why Dawg?!" Lump yelled with spit flying out of his mouth. "I don't know what y'all talking about." Responds T. B.G. smacks T again with the gun. "Tie this motherfucker up, and then sit him in that chair by the table, turn him around to face me." Said B.G. before continuing, "Get that dish towel over there and put it in his mouth."

B.G. smacks T again with the gun in the back of his head, and this time T's screams are silent. "Now, when you scream, can't nobody hear you. I'mma ask you a question and I'mma take the rag out your mouth for you to answer. If you lie, I'mma put the rag back in and we gone torture you. Who was that shooting at us?' Asked B.G taking the rag out of T's mouth. "I don't know." Answers T. Unsatisfied with his answer B.G.

195

instantly smacks T once again, and again the towel silenced his scream.

Lump grabs the large bag that he carried in on his shoulder. He opens it, pulling out a baseball bat. Seeing the bat, T's eyes grow wide. Bat in his hand Lump looks T straight into his eyes. "Why?" Lump asked again. Not yet looking for an answer, Lump swings at T's knee-caps with all of his might. The sounds of bones breaking can be heard. Lump cocked the bat back again.

"My best friend in the muthafuckin hospital. Why!?" B.G. yanks the towel out of T's mouth and T begins to speak. "The Mexicans, they on my line! They threatened to kill my family. If I didn't find out who took their shit, and killed the Plugs brother." Melvo was livid and didn't try to hide it. "So instead of you telling us so we can handle them together, you sold us out to them?" Melvo shook his head and walked away he couldn't stand the sight of this nigga.

"Who the fuck was that shooting at us mane?! If you say you don't know one more time, I'mma cut yo motherfucking ear off." Said B.G. T's eyes become much bigger. "It was either the Mexicans, or the police." Answered T. "Police... Tell me about this police." Responded B.G. "He's dirty. He works for the Mexicans." Lump said, "What's his name?!"

"Brooks." Melvo turned back around and bent down to look at T eye level, "That's the one who been at the hospital when all this shit been happening." B.G. then said, "Call him." Throwing the phone in his lap "They gon kill my family." Answered T. Slightly amused Lewis then said, "We gone kill yo family if you don't do what we want fool!"

Lump cut in, "You suppose to be Alla's father's man." Lump places the pistol to T's head. B.G. grabs Lump's hand. "We ain't finished yet, calm down and think. Right now we need him and he need us to keep his family alive…" B.G. looks into Lump's eyes and Lump understood the play that his father is laying down.

"Look motherfucker. We gone help you save your family. We want to get to the Mexicans. Do you have a way to get in touch with them?" Asked B.G. T responded, "I get in touch with them through Brooks." B.G. looks at Lump and then turned back to T, "Keep talking mane!" Breathing heavily, "Brooks is on their payroll. I was trying to find out who hit the lick, and when y'all came to me about moving the Ki's, I knew it was y'all." "You got to call Brooks and get him to come over here, so we can put pressure on him to get to the Mexicans. Look at me. We gon make sure your family safe first, then we gon take care of them." Ended B.G.

Melvo stepped up to T, "Are you with it or what nigga?" T held his head low unable to look at the young lion who he'd betrayed in his face, "Yeah, I'll help." Lump handed T his own phone off the floor that had fallen from his lap, and T began to dial Brook's cellular phone number. "Tell him you got Ru-boi, and you got info out of him, and how to get all of them at once."

When Brooks answered the phone, T said exactly what B.G. told him too, and Brooks said that he was on his way over to T's house. B.G. said, "Aiight, look mane, take that mini-van and move it so he don't think something up when he get here. He gon have to open the door- B.G. pointed at T while talking.

Lewis cut in, "He can't walk, you cracked his leg fool." He turns to Lump and laughs. B.G. then continued, "Well, stand his ass up at the door, he got to be at the door to get this nigga in. Lewis, you got to be behind the door to grab this nigga Brooks when he come in. We got to time this shit just right."

1 HOUR LATER

Pulling up to T's house, unaware of what is going on inside, Brooks jumps out of his car and heads to the front door. He paid no attention to the way that the curtains are pulled tight.

Brooks knocks on the door, and thirty seconds later, T opened the door. Stepping inside of the house Brooks began to speak, "Damn man, I almost had… Lewis bear hugs Brooks pinning his arms to his sides, B.G grabs his Glock from his holster. Lump let's go of T, and T instantly falls down to the floor. With Brooks' gun in his hand, B.G. orders Brooks to sit down inside of the chair that's sitting in the middle of the floor.

"Tie this motherfucker up fool! You the motherfucker that was shooting at us huh? You missed." Said B.G. Ru-boi and Melvo use the rope that Lewis and B.G. purchased from the hardware store. Lewis grabbed the glass jar that be brought, and said to the group, "I'm going to the bathroom."

B.G. grimaced, "You hunting for my boys huh?" Brooks responded, "I'm a Detroit Police Officer!" The looks on everybody's face told him they weren't impressed. "We know who you are. I guess you also and enforcer for the Mexicans. How that work? One hour you a police and the next you an enforcer. We gon keep this shit real short. Which one of you got the direct connect to the Mexicans?" B.G. asked. T answered, "I told you he do." T pointed to Brooks. Brooks responded, "Shut up!" Looking over at T, "If we don't need you, we might as well get rid of you now." Said B.G.

Raising the gun up to his head, B.G looked inside of Brooks' eyes and he could see the fear. In a shaky voice, Brooks answered, "Alright, I work for them, I can get in touch with them."

Hearing those words, Lump quickly grabbed a hold of one of the pillows off the couch and walked over to T. He places the pillow over T's face, stuffing his .40 caliber into the pillow to muffle the noise a little before he begins squeezing the trigger emptying two slugs into T's face.

B.G looked at Brooks and could see that he has piss stains on his pants. "Don't make us not need you. I'm willing to let you live and take your chances on the run from the Mexicans. I need to know where they at so we can finish this shit." Said B.G. to Brooks. "You can't finish this, it's too many of them." scoffed Brooks.

"Let's start by telling me what they know."
"They know it was some young black boys who took their shit, and killed their people, one of them big boy's brother." Said Brooks "Do they know their names?"
"No, we been dealing with all that."
"Who is we?"
"Me, him-
He looked down at T's body.
"And Hector?"
"He's another police who works with me."

Lump then cuts in, "Is he Mexican? Is he the one who shot Alla? They said it was some Mexicans who got out the van and shot him. Did this nigga Hector do it?" Brooks answers, "Yeah."
"Where is he?"
"He…
"Nigga where is he?!"
"He went to the hospital."
"Call Deuce and put him to point. Tell him to let Heather know."

Melvo pulled out his cellular phone. Lewis came walking from the bathroom with the jar in his hand. Lump, Melvo, and Ru-boi looked at Lewis. Lump started, "What the fuck you gon do with that Uncle Lewis?" B.G. began laughing a crazy sounding laugh. "Mane, this some down south North Memphis shit fool." Said B.G.

Lewis grabbed a row of nails for the nail gun. He then grabbed some latex gloves and put them on. Grabbing the jar and taking the top off, a foul smell instantly filled the room, as the aroma of piss and shit mixed in the jar hit the air…
Lewis began putting the nails inside of the mixture, then he placed the nails into the nail gun. B.G. began, "This shit give a motherfucker gangrene when you shoot a nigga with it. Lewis like this kind of shit mane." Brooks shouted, "I told y'all I would help, you don't need to use that on me!"

B.G. said, "Good, then well use it on the Mexicans. See how that work fool. Now we got a understanding. Tell me more about these Mexicans. Where they at, how many of them is it, what kind of guns they got. I want to know all this shit." As Brooks begins to speak, everybody gave their attention to get all of the details. They couldn't afford to slip. The Mexicans don't play…

DETROIT RECEIVING

As the male nurse walked through the hospital hallways, he didn't notice that Detective Campbell was trailing behind him. Walking towards Allante's room, He passed the mother's sitting in the waiting area. Approaching the nurses' station, the head nurse looks at him, and began to intercept him however he is waved off by Campbell.

Arriving at the door, he places his left hand on the door, and softly pushes it open. Seeing only Heather's back as she sits at Allante's side, he reached for his waist and fully entered the room. The door closed behind him, he takes a step forward, the cold tip of the gun barrel was felt on the back of his head. Deuce said seductively, "We been waiting on you bitch."

Heather turns around in the chair and you can see her hand on the trigger of her Glock as it laid in her waist. Getting up from the chair, she points the gun straight at Hector's face. Tears coming out of her eyes, she began to speak, "He's in this damn bed because of you. I hate your motherfucking ass, I'mma blow your motherfucking brains out!"

The room doors open up and Campbell walks inside with her gun pointed. Campbell began, "Washington! Lower your gun. I got it now…" Deuce responded, "Nawl, fuck this nigga ole dirty police he came in here to kill Alla." With her voice as cold as her glare speaking through her clenched teeth. "Dirty police get taken in, but my boyfriend is in Intensive Care." Said Heather.

"Young lady, if you kill him, you will go to jail." You could be with him for all I know so "I don't want to hear that shit, how we know you ain't dirty?" Heather spewed. While the three of them talked, Hector reached for his gun and one shot was fired to his head, led his body to fall to the ground. Head hitting the floor, his blood streamed from the side of his head…

T'S HOUSE

Brooks is talking, "Yeah Joker, we got the other two. We caught them coming out of the hospital visiting the one Hector shot. Look, it's real tight right now with all of the shootings going on right now…. No, we're not going over there. We'll meet you at 1713 West Outer Drive. Bring my money and bring the groceries for T. We can take care of all of this at one time. This is a Residential neighborhood, so we'll meet at 1:30 tonight. People will be sleep and the cars won't draw attention."

B.G. asked, "Lil nigga, why you give them that address?" Lump answered, "that's a house me, Melvo, and Allante' were working on buying. We ain't getting that shit now. But it's a perfect spot for us to rock these motherfuckers to sleep at because it's an upscale neighborhood, they won't expect nothing." Smiling a wide gold toothed grin B.G. said to his son, "Good thinking lil fool. You got some of me in you after all." Lump smiled as B.G. places one arm around him and pulled him close.

"Daddy, we gon have to get over there early so we can have shit set up. Plus, they might send some people over there to scope the spot out." Melvo added. "Damn, what you lil niggas need us to come up here for, y'all know what y'all doing. Shit, y'all should come on back with me and run shit back down at home." Said B.G. Lump half-smiled, "We gon cook this beef up here first Daddy, we gon lay down some shit they ain't gone never forget."

Pointing at T, Lump then continued, "Ru-boi, go get the van so we can put this bitch ass motherfucker body in it. Make sure you back your way up the drive-way so the sliding door of the van be right in front of the side door of the house. We got to wipe this motherfucking house down where we been at." Melvo looked around the room, "That ain't gon be hard fool. We only been in the living room and the kitchen. Oh yeah, and Lewis was in the bathroom…" He laughed.

B.G. turns to Brooks, "Don't fuck this up. So far so good. If I think you gon cross us in any way, I'mma let Lewis deal with you. You rather have a bullet shot up your ass then to have Lewis get on one of his torture trips. I'm telling you right now he's on some real gruesome shit. Let him smell that shit Lewis." Lewis opens the jar placing it under Brooks' nose, and B.G. instantly let out that crazy ass laugh of his.

BACK INSIDE THE HOSPITAL ROOM

Campbell demanded, "Put that goddamn gun away! Look, people are going to come in this room in any minute now. Please listen to me and put that gun away!" Heather snapped out of her trance as she looked down at Hector's lifeless body. Turning to Deuce, Campbell demanded, "You too! Put you gun up Washington! "Now when they come in here, you were sitting in the chair by Allante', the officer had his gun pointed at you when

Washington and I came in that's when I shot him. Do you got it?" In shock both Heather and Deuce respond with nods of their heads.

Seconds later, hospital security came running through the door followed by the hospital staff, and the three mothers. Campbell began, "I'm Detective Bernice Campbell. This is now a crime scene. I need everybody to step out of this room. You, security make sure this area is clear, and only let Detroit police enter this area. Mrs. Light your son was uninjured, please trust me and let me do my job."

Deborah nodded head, and stepped out of the room with the rest of the mothers'. Campbell turns to Heather and Deuce, "How did y'all know who he was?" Deuce answered, "We got a call that a hit was coming." Campbell's adrenaline was still pumping. "Who did you get the call from?" Deuce smirked and waved her off, "What da fuck we look like tellin' you that and you got dirty police trying to kill us."

Campbell pulled out her cellular phone and began dialing her partner's number. "Brooks, when you get this call, call me. I'm at Detroit Receiving, get here ASAP." Campbell ended her call, and then she went on to tell the two teens to get rid of their guns but not to leave the hospital. One by one the two teens walked out of the room and up to

Mrs. Armstrong sliding her the two guns. Mrs. Armstrong slipped out of the hospital and put the two guns in here vehicle.

LUMP ON HIS CELLULAR PHONE

"Hello? Are y'all aiight? What about Alla?" Lump glared at Brooks with murder in his eyes before continuing, "Just make sure you, Alla, and Deuce straight... We'll be there once we finish taking care of this business..."

After ending his phone call with Heather, Lump turns to his crew. "His man tried to hit Allante', Heather and Deuce had him and he went for his gun..." Lump looked at Brooks, "Your bitch shot him, and he's dead."

MELVO

"Look mane, we gotta go. We got to end this shit. I want to see these niggas." Said Melvo. B.G. asked, "What he suppose to be bringing?" Brooks answered, "My money he owe me for all of them, and the shipment of Ki's for T."
"How many Ki's?" Asked B.G.
"A hundred."
B.G. whistles then spoke, "We gon kill these

motherfuckers and hit a lick. Shit, I might move up this motherfucker. What you say Lewis?" he laughed wickedly. Lewis smiled, "Let's kill these motherfuckers and then talk about it nigga."

1713 WEST OUTER DRIVE
1:30 A.M.

Two black Cadillac Escalades pull up in front of the house. "I want to see these motherfuckers face when we torture them. And I want you to kill them slowly in the worse way." Said the plug, Puncho Diaz. Joker added, "Don't worry, I'll make sure fear is spread, and the message is clear, not to fuck with us! What about the police and the one whose family we threatened?"

"Kill them too, we don't need them anymore either. We'll find another distributor, that won't be hard. Come on, let's get this shit over with." Joker then got on his cell phone. Five seconds later two Mexicans got out of the first Escalade approaching the back doors of the second Escalade for Puncho and Joker to get out.

They methodically walk up to the house surrounded by five other Mexicans totaling seven in all, Joker looked up at the second level of the house. Standing in the window, Melvo extended his arm and intentionally moved the curtains. Just enough to draw their attention to where he stood upstairs; it worked just as planned.

The Mexican fools never noticed B.G, Lewis, and Ru-boi dressed in all black, with ski-masks creeping up from both sides of the house and also from the back. Running down on the Mexicans, like Navy Seals on a special ops mission, B.G., Lewis, and Ru-boi had their weapons at the low and ready firing position.

Hands on the triggers, the three-man crew began to squeeze their triggers at the same time, rapid rounds of three and a half inch nails penetrated the heads of four of the seven men. Very few people understand the force that a nail gun can produce. These three and a half inch nails become a deadly weapon in the hands of a determined killer... Six or seven nails found their mark in the heads of the poor men that the crew aimed to knock down.

The nails pierced the air in perfect silence. The bodies dropped, the other three Mexicans stood standing still obviously stunned at the swiftness of the killers who are now right up on them. B.G. and Lewis squeezed four rounds apiece into the shoulders of two of the remaining three. The move was done to make them think twice about reaching for their weapons...

LUMP

Lump opened the front door with his Glock in his hand. He reaches into the waistline of the three remaining Mexicans to disarm them of their guns. Telling the three men to get into the house, Lump began to take control. B.G. stood looking proudly knowing that his seeds have both become young men.

They were young lions indeed, and they were about to feast on their prey. Lump said, "Melvo come'ere, you grab that body right there. Ru-boi grab that one, and Daddy I need you to get that one." Grabbing the four dead bodies and pulling them inside the house, Lump closed the door behind them. He said, "Check them niggas and make sho they all dead. Ru-boi, I'm pretty sure, but go out to the back patio and creep to those Escalades and make sure ain't nobody else in them."

Brooks spoke, "I'll go with him." Lump responded, "Fuck nawl nigga, you stay RIGHT HERE!" Lewis said, "I'll go, I got you young nigga." Turning to Puncho, Joker, and the last flunky, Lump asked, "Which one of you is the plug?" Nodding his head with confidence, "I am." Answered Puncho. Lump stared and pointed at Joker, "So you the enforcer?" Joker hesitantly nods his head. Lump continues, "Aiight, you two move." Lump leads Puncho and Joker downstairs into the basement. Melvo and Brooks went down in front of them. Lump said, "Tie them bitch ass muthafuckas up tight both hands, and feet!"

Puncho said, "You're making a mistake."
"Nawl motherfucker you made the mistake. Don't
say shit else or I'mma take this baseball bat and
bust your motherfucking face wide open!" Said
Lump. Puncho immediately closed his mouth.
"Put tape over their mouths so they can't talk to
each other." After their mouths were taped, Lump
said, "Come on y'all let's go upstairs and see this
flunky up here. I know he don't wanna die, he'll
tell us what we need to know." Ru-boi came back
into the house, "Both them trucks are empty
homey. The front one got a rack of Ki's and some
black bags in it."

Lump looked over at Melvo and nods his
head, "You deal wit'em fool. Maybe he wanna
live." Melvo responds, "What's your name mane?"
Stuttering the Mexican answered, "Ru--Rudy."
"That almost sound like Ru-boi." The crew
laughed trying to ease the Mexicans nerves. Melvo
continued, "Rudy, believe me, they gon die. We
not gon let them live. Bet you, you can get away
cause wont nobody know that you are alive, do
you wanna live?"

Nodding his head very quickly. Rudy
responded, "Si amigo!" Melvo asked him, "How
many more of y'all is it?" Looking around the
room as he spoke unsure of just who to speak
directly to, "It's about six that we left at the house
in Southwest Detroit, but they're nobodies they

don't even speak English. They're not leaders, and without Puncho and Joker they're completely lost." Melvo then says, "What's my name?" Rudy shrugs his shoulders before saying, "I don't know Amigo. They don't give us your names. No details. We are only as you would say, Foot Soldiers." "That's too bad." Melvo called Ru-boi over and whispered into his ear.

Ru-boi told the Mexican to come on and he led him out onto the back patio. There, Ru-boi emptied seven mails into the Mexicans head. Melvo told him to do it out of the sight of Brooks because they didn't want to spook him. There was still something that they had to be sure of. Ru-boi pulled the body into the kitchen leaving it there on the kitchen floor. Lump walked up, "Let's finish this shit."

Lump led the way back downstairs to the basement. Standing next to Brooks with a nail gun in his hands, Melvo looked directly into the directly into the eyes of the two Mexicans, and began speaking to Brooks. "So, Brooks, if we kill these muthafuckas right here, and leave their bodies we all can walk away and go back to living?"

"I never told them your names. They didn't even ask. They just wanted revenge. Me and T were just to suppose to get it done. Once we got

212

y'all, we were supposed to make an example out of y'all." Raising his hand, Melvo shot three nails into the side of Brooks' head and his body fell sideways to the basement floor, Melvo then bent down and placed the nail gun to the side of Brooks' face and began to empty the nails into Brooks face nailing his head to the floor. Brooks didn't have a face anymore, all you could see were the nails where his face once was. Turning his face to the Mexicans, Melvo grits his teeth, "We know how to make examples out of muthafuckas too!"

Looking at the gruesome scene, the two Mexicans bent their heads down looking to the ground knowing that their lives were over. Lump stepped back to the front, and the Mexicans lifted their heads to look at him. Lump began, "My father wants to torture y'all. I want to do more than torture y'all. I want to set y'all muthafuckas on fire. Maybe over there in Mexico, they scared of y'all. Niggas die over here just like over there. We got gangs over here too, we got shootouts over here too. And we murder muthafuckas just like y'all. I know young niggas who got bodies at the age of thirteen. So nawl, we ain't scared of none of you muthafuckas. Your brother got killed? Well, that shit shouldn't of been in our neighborhood without us eatin' too…PERIOD!" Lump lifts the nail gun, shooting Puncho and then Joker in their knee caps. Both men made muffled screams because of the duct-tape over their mouths.

Melvo grabbed the same baseball bat from earlier and beat both the men with it on their knees crushing their knee caps. Lump pointed the nail gun at the groin area of Puncho and fired a couple of nails hitting him all in his dick and nuts. B.G. let out a crazy laugh. Melvo took the bat and raised it like a baseball player swinging with all of his might crashing the bat into Joker's face.

Blood splattered everywhere. Melvo began, "That's for my nigga Alla! Yeah, we killed your brother! Bitch! Now we gon kill you!" B.G stepped in grabbing the bat from his son. "Y'all did enough mane, let me and Lewis handle it from here." Said B.G. Lump cut in, "But daddy!" B.G. stated, "Lump, I got it. We got it! Go check on Allante'. Me and Lewis about to have some fun fool!"

As Lump, Melvo, and Ru-boi walked up the basement steps, B.G. could be heard telling Lewis to hand him some honey and a jar of ants. The three boys placed their black hoodies over their heads walking to the first escalade getting inside of it. Ru-boi handed Lump the keys that he had taken out of the pocket of the dead Mexican who they shot at the front door of the house. Lump put the keys into the ignition, started the vehicle up, and they pulled off. Melvo began, "Let's unload this shit and get rid of this Escalade before we go back to the hospital fool." Lump responded, "What we

gon do with all this shit?" Melvo laughed, "Nigga what you mean shiiiiiiit, we gon keep the money and split it between the five of us. We'll give Daddy the Ki's and tell him to break us off our cut when he sell them." He dapped his brother up, "Fool, you a muthafucka!" Said Lump.
Melvo responded, "Nawl fool, you a muthafucka." Ru-boi added, "We all MOTHERfuckas homey!" The three young boys laughed on their way to stash the money and the Ki's.

3 DAYS LATER
COBO HALL

"And the class of 2017 now calls, Allante' Light!" Thunderous sounds of clapping and loud cheering could be heard as the students of Northwestern High School stand to their feet and began clapping. Arraja and Andre Light walked across the stage followed by Mrs. Light to receive Allante' diploma. Allante' still lay in the hospital recovering from his wounds.

Across town, in Southwest Detroit, the police approach the black escalade using the sleeves of their shirts to cover their noses and block out the foul smell arising from the escalade. As they opened the door, the smell from the dead bodies was unbearable for the officers to stand. Several dead Mexicans lay inside of the luxury truck, their bodies decomposing. The message was clear. Joker's body laid in the back of the Escalade naked. His dick was cut off and stuffed up his ass. The Mexicans were known for cutting off a man's dick and putting it into a man's mouth. B.G. and Lewis took it a step further and took Joker's dick stuffing it up his ass hole with a broom stick. Boy oh boy Lewis was a twisted motherfucker. Puncho's body lay naked, and the police looked shocked as they observed the tortured corpse. All of his fingertips were burned as if he had been put under a fire. The blow-torch left the cooked affect as if his fingertips had been roasted. Dried up blood around his moth revealed that his tongue was missing. But the most gruesome thing of all was that apparently honey was smeared all over Puncho's nuts and ass and ants were poured all over the honey because of this the ants had eaten Puncho's nuts and asshole.

The message was clear... Whoever killed these men were saying, "WE WANT TO TURN IT UP TEN TIMES!" T's body lay in the back of the S.U.V. as well as Brooks' faceless body. The young lions weren't bullshitting, and whoever would be the next plug would get the message loud and clear. DON'T COME IN DETROIT ACTING LIKE YOU RUN SHIT. IF WE DON'T EAT, NEITHER DO YOU!" That was DEFINITELY the message that Allante' was trying to send.

DETROIT RECEIVING HOSPITAL

Heather sit's inside of the cushioned chair beside Allante's bed. She and Mrs. Light have been switching hours and days of sitting by his side so that Heather could finish graduating High School and Cosmetology school. While sitting by Allante's bed, a knock was heard on the room's door. Heather turned to face to the room door, and she watched as 6'2 tall white man came inside.

Straightening up in the chair, she looked at the man who began to speak. "Hello, my name is Gerald Lawrence, and I'm Allante's attorney. I take it you name is Heather, Heather Brown?"
"Yes, that's my name.'
"I'm sorry to meet you under such terms, but Allante' wrote this letter and told me to give it to you if anything were to happen to him. He is very exceptional for his age. How are you holding up?"
"I just wish he would wake up."
"He's a fighter, and a good one. If you need anything, you contact me. I'm your lawyer also. He paid me to be retained for the both of you."
"Thank you." She reached out her hand and the two shook hands. Lawrence gave her a business card along with the letter before walking out of the room. Looking at the envelope inside of her hand, she sat back in the chair, opened the envelope, pulled the letter out and began to read...

"Hello beautiful.

If you are reading this letter, either I'm hurt, or I'm not there anymore. I hope it's just something wrong with me ☺ Laugh girl! When I saw you the first time, I was caught off guard by this sexy, pretty brown skinned young flower. The first look at you still stays in my mind like practice taken and kept for memories. I knew you would be mines because I couldn't see myself being without you. Talking to you over the phone and hearing you talk about your dreams allowed me to see your heart and your passion. I fell in love with you, and I fell in love with your dreams as well. Loving you made me want to make your dreams come true. You're a Queen and I try to treat you like one. I believe that making love to you was like entering heaven. And therefore you are my heaven on earth. I'm sorry that I have not fulfilled my promise to you, but I have put things in place to make sure you fulfill your dreams-

Heather begins crying before she continues to read the letter, "I brought some security bonds and put

them in you and Josh's name. They add up to
about $100,000.00 dollars. I put $150,000.00 in
that paper bag for you to put in the Security
Deposit box. And it's over $3,000,000.00 million
dollars in my storage unit. The house was written off
as a gift inheritance, and put in both of our names,
I just didn't tell you. So, I need you to do me
some favors beautiful. My mother wouldn't take
any money from me, so I need you to look out for
her and my little brothers. Make sure they don't
have to do what I did. Make sure they know I
love them. Look out for my boys. Lump and
Melvo won't need my money, but my love for
them they can always use. Keep in touch with
them for me, and if they stray, say my name.
Always be their friend and let them know you got
their back. Open up a Beauty Salon, you're
going to make it. And live life to the fullest.
Don't ever let a sucker play you or mistreat you.
I set a standard of how you should be treated and
loved. Don't settle for less, and don't be a sucker

for love. Know your worth and remember me. Just know that I love you, and I'm always with you. Love young Lion... Allante'.

Heather cried profusely as she read the letter and put her head between her folded arms on Allante's bed. After crying for about two minutes a soft voice said, "What you crying for?" Raising her head in disbelief, Heather looks into Allante's opened eyes and with joy in her heart, she spoke, "You came back to me! Oh my God! You came back to me..." Allante' spoke, "My body is sore as shit." Wiping her tears, "I'mma take care of you, don't worry.' Said Heather.

"Where's Lump and Melvo?" Allante' looked around. "I'll call them, you been sleep for a while. I got to call your mother." Heather frantically searched her pockets for her phone "You been by my side?" he smiled weakly. "All the time. I'mma always be by your side. It's over. All of it. Lump and Melvo finished it." "Is everybody okay?" she nodded but in agreement but he could see that she still looked sad. "T, he set you up, and the police were involved." "What about our families?" Rubbing his face, she said, "Baby, everybody is okay, get your rest. I love you." Allante' cleared his throat, "I love you more." Heather climbed up on the bed and lay next to Allante', blessed that her love had come back to her. She would nurse him back to good health and he would be a helluva father to Josh and their baby.

The game comes with a price, it's all about who's going to pay for it.

1 YEAR LATER

The bass of music filled the air so Heather spoke loudly, "Allante' would you come here please?" Keisha then said, "Girl, he over there talking up a storm. Look at them, they all animated and shit." Heather turned back to her friends, "He better not let that food burn on that grill. I spent all day yesterday going all over the east and west side to get that meat and then I had to prepare it so it could marinate over night. He always be bragging, talking about he can cook better than me, he swear he a Chef." Heather laughed hysterically.

The girls began laughing too while they sat at the patio table in Heather and Allante's backyard. The pride is back together as Allante' is cooking on the grill talking to Lump, Melvo, Ru-boi, and Deuce. Lump spoke, "Hey fool, Heather just called you. You know you a daddy now. She probably want you to change shorty's diaper and shit." All of the friends laughed. Allante' and Heather had a beautiful baby boy name Courtland. Flipping the meat on the grill Allante asked Melvo "So, when you gonna have the first line of shirts out, and what do the jeans look like?" Rubbing his hands together as he spoke, "Nigga you better be on some fly shit!" Melvo responded, "I'mma bring the first designer shirts out next week. They tough as hell. Mo, y'all gonna love this shit. All the ballers gonna be rocking it. Watch and see. I got shit for all incomes. I don't want to leave out people who ain't got it like that. We wasn't always rich." Lump adds, "Yeah but fool, we richer than a motherfucker now."

"Nawl, but straight up Mo, I'm proud as hell of you. You made that shit come true." Said Allante'. "You said we needed a plan Alla, we did it. Rich young niggas..." Replied Melvo. Although he's currently still attending Fashion Design College, Melvo has already started his very own clothing line. He almost let his father talk him into calling it Vernace, and use an African Prairie dog as the logo. Luckily Lump and Allante' laughed him out of those plans and he snapped out of it. He named the clothing line, B.G.I., which stands for Been Getting It. There is already a buzz that they created on all of the fashion blogs and social media sites waiting for his debut.

Lump began, "Alla, we got some fly ass whips that we bought being delivered on the lot tomorrow, what time you coming in?" Briefly looking in the sky, Uh I'll be there about 10:30 or so cause I gotta go down to the City County building to check on the deed for this building in the Cass Corridor. This might be our first building Mo." Allante' beamed with pride. Lump and Allante' went into business together. They got their mothers to take out a loan for them and they started a used car lot. Coincidently; they called the lot, Dreams, because they set out to make people's dreams come true of owning a car. They went to the police auction and started buying up all the luxury cars that were confiscated during drug forfeitures.

Together they purchased a small lot, put a wrought iron fence around it, then had a little office built on the property. Now they have their own dealership with filled luxury vehicles ranging from BMW, Mercedes Benz, Jaguar, and Cadillac's on their lot. True to the plan they worked with people in the hood who didn't have the best credit. They have put plenty of single mother's in the cars of their dreams.

The trio also opened up a Real Estate company. They bought a couple of empty lots and abandoned properties close to downtown. Their theory is that as the city begins to build and become revitalized those lots and abandoned properties will become high-end real estate ventures and maybe they will build something on them and sell to the highest bidder.

Allante' also has a separate Real Estate business where he purchased seven houses at a land-bank foreclosure auction. He hired some old drug addicts to help him fix them up and he either sells them or rents them to women who can't afford loans from banks. The young pride has done well, and their bond is stronger than any other force known to man. They truly are a family.

Heather spoke, "Watch this bitch." Heather stands up carrying Courtland over to Allante'. The two pit bull puppies Lady and Gentleman, who are now one year old followed her over to where the young men are. "Your son is calling you Daddy." Said Heather playfully.
"I got you beautiful. I always got you." Allante' smacked Heather on her ass and she turned around walking back over to her girls. She switched her ass with more intent after Allante' smacked it and her girlfriends laughed as she winked her eye at them.

Since Allante' came home from the hospital, Heather never left his side, making sure he went to all of his rehab appointments and just taking care of her man and best friend. Josh is two and a half years old now, and thinks the new edition to the family is his sole responsibility. Allante' keeps Josh by his side and has loved him like his own. Heather is planning her wedding and is living like she is in a dream. In one week she opens her first hair salon and the name of it is called "Another Level." She already has plans to open up another. She is a helluva business woman and her eyes are set on crushing everything she puts her mind on. When Allante' saw her, he knew there was no limit to her success.

Young, black, gifted, and dangerous, from young boys to true natural born hustlers, Allante', Melvo, and Lump are legends, and they are just beginning. Yeah, It Comes With A Price, because if you fuck with the crew of young lions, your ass it out. Ask Puncho....

Coming out of the movie theater, Allante' put his right arm around Heather's shoulders and pulled her close. She leaned into him and began to speak, "That was one of the best movies I ever saw baby." He laughed and said, "All of y'all girls love a happy ending." Allante' he stopped and turned her towards him taking in all of her beauty they shared a kiss. Allante' stepped back and said to his fiancé "I can't even lie Heather ...that shit was fire...and I know it's gon be one so just wait till Part 2 comes out, it's gon be a motherfucker!"